Destiny's Bride

Also by Jane Peart in Large Print:

Autumn Encore
Folly's Bride
Fortune's Bride
Gallant Bride
Love Takes Flight
Ransomed Bride
Sandcastles
Scent of Heather
Sign of the Carousel
A Sinister Silence
Valiant Bride
Yankee Bride/Rebel Bride:
   Montclair Divided

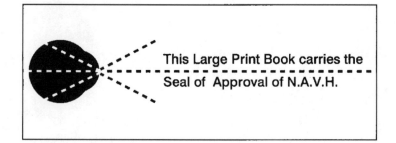

The Brides of Montclair
Book 8

Destiny's Bride

Jane Peart

Thorndike Press • Waterville, Maine

Published in 2005 by arrangement with
Natasha Kern Literary Agency, Inc.

Thorndike Press® Large Print Christian Romance.

The tree indicium is a trademark of Thorndike Press.

The text of this Large Print edition is unabridged.
Other aspects of the book may vary from the original edition.

Set in 16 pt. Plantin by Carleen Stearns.

Printed in the United States on permanent paper.

Library of Congress Cataloging-in-Publication Data

Peart, Jane.
    Destiny's bride / by Jane Peart.
       p. cm. — (The Brides of Montclair series ; bk. 8)
(Thorndike Press large print Christian romance)
    ISBN 0-7862-7823-4 (lg. print : hc : alk. paper)
    1. Plantation owners' spouses — Fiction.
2. Williamsburg Region (Va.) — Fiction.   3. Plantation life
— Fiction.   4. Large type books.   5. Domestic fiction.
I. Title.   II. Thorndike Press large print Christian romance
series.
PS3566.E238D47 2005
813'.54—dc22   2005010542

For my sisters,
Ruth and Audrey,
who shared my childhood —
the love, laughter, tears and triumphs!

National Association for Visually Handicapped
---------------------- *serving the partially seeing*

As the Founder/CEO of NAVH, the only national health agency solely devoted to those who, although not totally blind, have an eye disease which could lead to serious visual impairment, I am pleased to recognize Thorndike Press* as one of the leading publishers in the large print field.

Founded in 1954 in San Francisco to prepare large print textbooks for partially seeing children, NAVH became the pioneer and standard setting agency in the preparation of large type.

Today, those publishers who meet our standards carry the prestigious "Seal of Approval" indicating high quality large print. We are delighted that Thorndike Press is one of the publishers whose titles meet these standards. We are also pleased to recognize the significant contribution Thorndike Press is making in this important and growing field.

Lorraine H. Marchi, L.H.D.
Founder/CEO
NAVH

* Thorndike Press encompasses the following imprints: Thorndike, Wheeler, Walker and Large Print Press.

Part I
September 1882

Excerpts from the journal of
Druscilla Montrose

1881–1884

chapter
1

"Dru! Druscilla!" My mother's voice startled me awake. She was bending over me, her expression so distressed that I felt a pang of alarm.

I raised myself on my elbows, rubbing the sleep from my eyes. "What is it, Mama?"

"Oh, my dear, we have just had the most dreadful news. Alair is dead!" Her wide dark eyes grew suddenly bright with tears.

Fully awake now, I sat up. "Dead! Alair? But how?" My cousin was only twenty-six, just six years older than I, and in the prime of radiant young womanhood.

"We don't know all the details. We just got word. Some kind of accident." She began turning back the bedcovers. "You must get up at once. There really is no time to lose, Dru. We must leave Mayfield as soon as possible. Garnet will send a carriage to meet us at the station."

Mama's hands shook as she handed me a

cup of coffee to drink while I tried to absorb this shattering news.

"I must arrange for Auntie Nell's care while we are gone. Poor soul, she's quite distraught, but at her age the train trip and funeral would be too much. Now, hurry, dear! I've sent Bessie to the train station to see when the next train is leaving, and we must be on it!"

My mother left the room and I got shakily to my feet. I couldn't seem to gather my wits. All that had registered was the stunning announcement that my cousin was dead!

I glanced at my open trunk, half-packed, standing in the corner. I was to leave for my new teaching post at Thornycroft School in Massachusetts at the end of the week. Dazed, I moved toward it. Had I packed anything that would be suitable for a funeral?

Funeral! Alair's funeral. The unreality of it rolled over me in a fresh wave of grief, and I was wrenched back eight years to a happier day. I could hear Alair's voice.

"But of course, Druscilla's going to be in my wedding! She will wear the loveliest dress of pink ruffled lawn with a pink satin sash, and carry pink roses. It will be perfect with her dark hair and beautiful eyes.

10

Oh, Aunt Dove, you can't say no!"

If there had been any doubt in Mama's mind that I should be one of Alair's bridal attendants, it vanished in that moment. No one had ever been able to deny Alair anything she was set on having. I never quite understood why.

Even at twelve, I knew Alair's engagement to Randall Bondurant had caused a flurry of controversy throughout our plantation community. There had been strong feelings as to whether or not any of our family should even attend the wedding, much less participate in it.

I remember the buzz of speculation among the older family members when the announcement came.

"Not suitable at all!"

"Well, he *is* from an old Charleston family —"

"But disowned, I'm told."

"Something about a duel?"

"No, but he was expelled from the Citadel —"

"Some boyish prank, I suppose?"

"Gambling, my dear!"

Shocked gasps all around.

"Besides, he's ten years older —"

"And as rich as Croesus." The last uttered with a certain respect.

"What do Harmony and Clinton say?"

"What *can* they say? They've always spoiled the girl outrageously."

"Yes, she is willful and headstrong."

"But what can a young lady do in these times, these circumstances?"

Again, a round of heavy sighing.

"The truth and pity of it is that so many of our gallant young men perished in the War."

"The War!" There was a consensus of nods. Then someone had said, "Well, at least, she will live at Montclair."

"Bon-Chance," corrected another.

"Good Luck, indeed!" was the final cryptic comment.

I knew that the reason for all the debate was an old family scandal, one that was spoken of in whispers . . . although it was an open secret in Mayfield.

Randall Bondurant now lived on the estate that had been Montrose property for generations, ever since it was built on an original King's Grant in the 1700s, until it was lost to Bondurant by my Uncle Malcolm in a card game.

I had grown up at Montclair with my cousins — Alair Chance and Jonathan Montrose — and our mothers, who decided to move in together for the sake of safety and joint strength while our fathers were off fighting in the War. So, of course, I was pleased when Bondurant restored the house and gardens to their antebellum splendor and was thrilled to learn that the wedding would be held there.

Certainly, Alair was beside herself with excitement, and even the name change didn't concern her in the least.

"I think it's absolutely the most romantic thing a man ever did!" she trilled as we were being fitted for our dresses. "To combine my last name and his for our new home! Oh, we shall be so happy. I know it! What's more —" She dimpled and winked in a conspiratorial manner — "I think I deserve some credit for getting the place back into the family . . . no matter what it's called!" And she tossed her beautiful head in the careless way she had.

At that point, I didn't care what our relatives said, either. I thought Randall Bondurant dashing and handsome, and that Alair was the luckiest girl in the world.

I adored Alair, always had ever since those days at Montclair when she had so often declared herself the leader of our trio, teasing Jonathan and me if we lagged behind in any of her reckless games — climbing trees, wading in the creek, playing in the woods. If she were our self-appointed "queen," the two of us were her willing subjects. And on the few occasions when we dared to question her leadership, she said she should lead because she was the oldest. Actually it was because she knew how to charm and manipulate to get her way even then, and we gladly agreed just for the privilege of playing with her.

Lost in my memories of those carefree days, I was still standing in my nightgown, my cup of untasted coffee in my hand, when Mama came back into the bedroom.

"Not dressed yet? Darling, do hurry. Our train leaves at one. Shall I help?"

"No, thank you, Mama, I'll manage. It's just that somehow I can't believe it yet — that Alair is really dead."

"I know, darling." Mama took the cup from me and set it down, then hugged me. "I understand just how you feel."

And I knew she did. Tragedy was no stranger to her. Loss, loneliness, poverty had been her lot. Raised in wealth, destined for a life of luxury and leisure, she had been widowed at twenty, her father's fortune wiped out. With a child to support, Dove Arundel Montrose had no choice but to survive.

She had taught school, worked as a

seamstress and now lived with our elderly relative, Nell Perry, as the old woman's housekeeper-companion. As I looked into my mother's once beautiful face, it seemed even lovelier to me than the pictures of her, painted when she was younger. Now there was an inner beauty shining through, the kind only strength, courage, and compassion can give.

"Now, dear, we really must hurry." She gave me another hug and left me to make my hasty preparations for the trip.

Although it was only early September, the day was overcast and a chill, sharp wind tugged at our skirts and whipped our bonnet strings as we followed the flower-banked casket up to the hilltop Montrose family graveyard above the house once known as Montclair.

Standing at Alair's gravesite in the Montrose family hilltop cemetery, I couldn't help thinking of the irony. The last time all the family had gathered was at her wedding eight years ago. Death seemed that much more cruel, to have taken one so young and so beautiful.

I looked at Alair's husband across the yawning chasm of the grave. Randall's head was bowed, his broad shoulders slumped. The two little girls stood on either side of him, holding his hands.

Alair's children, I thought, feeling my throat tighten. With their long fair hair and delicate features, they looked remarkably like her when she was a child. But the eyes — oh, the eyes were Bondurant's — large and dark, now filled with an expression of bewildered sadness. At seven and five, these little ones had no idea of the enormity of their loss.

Because Randall and Alair had traveled a great deal and because of our circumstances, I saw my cousin only rarely after her marriage. At first, she would appear unexpectedly at Montclair, fashionably dressed and bringing gifts and her own unique brand of *joie de vivre* that evoked so many fond remembrances. But not recently. None of us had seen Alair in nearly two years.

My eyes traveled around the group of mourners. Beside my mother stood Aunt Garnet, elegant in a black faille suit and wearing a stylish bonnet that did not completely hide her still-glorious red-gold hair. She had known her share of sorrow, even though she was now married to a wealthy publisher and kept houses in both New York and London. She had buried her first hero-husband — my Uncle Bryce — in this same cemetery. Surely she must be thinking of him today.

Next to Garnet was her mother, Kate Cameron — tall, regal, still beautiful in her sixties. I could detect few scars of the long hard years of struggle. I felt a rush of warmth. This woman had been like a grandmother to me. After the War, Kate had opened an exclusive school for young ladies in her home and asked Mama to be one of the teachers. So we moved to Cameron Hall, where I had been able to receive the same fine education and cultural advantages that the daughters of the "nouveau riche" Yankee families had to pay mightily for.

Then my eyes rested on the small, dignified figure of my mother, with her cameo features and silver hair. I saw the sympathy on her face as she looked at Randall and I followed her glance.

At that very moment he lifted his head, and I saw his eyes like two burning coals in his ravaged face. For a few seconds our gazes locked, and I saw the raw grief there. I drew in my breath. Then I saw something in his expression that frightened me — and I turned quickly away.

At last the service was over, and the line

of mourners filed through the black iron-lace gate of the cemetery fence, winding through velvety, manicured lawns back toward the mansion. I could not help thinking that these had been the untended meadows where Jonathan, Alair, and I had once romped and played.

By the time we arrived at the house, Bondurant and the children had disappeared up the steps. I swallowed my disappointment, I had so wanted to get a closer look at those forlorn little girls, perhaps offer them some comfort.

"Please try to understand. The man's broken-hearted." Uncle Clinton tried to explain. "It happened so suddenly that none of us —" He cleared his throat. "But you will come to our house, won't you? Harmony needs —" His voice trailed away as he looked toward his heavily veiled wife as she, supported by her maid, was being handed into their carriage.

"Of course, we understand, Clint." Garnet hushed him with a restraining hand on his arm. "We'll be along presently."

Once in her carriage on the way to the Chance home, however, she raised an eyebrow. "You would think Randall Bondurant might have stayed long enough to accept our condolences —"

"You heard Clinton, Garnet. He said Randall was too depressed to speak to anyone," Kate put in mildly.

"Yes, but we're family, after all."

"Well, we really have not been much family to him, my dear. None of us ever really accepted him," Kate reminded her. "Nor received him, for that matter."

Since the truth could not be disputed, no further comments were made.

As we rounded the bend of the drive leaving Montclair, I turned to look back. How I would have loved to have gone inside, walk through the house I had known so well as a child. It was a house where I had been very happy. I wondered if Alair had been happy there.

As I was taking that last lingering look, a sudden brisk wind sent a scatter of golden leaves spinning from the elm trees that lined the drive. I shivered. It seemed the symbol of the end of a golden era of my life. I felt I would never see my childhood home again.

chapter
2

The house Randall Bondurant had presented his new in-laws upon his marriage to
their daughter was impressive. I was more
than a little awed by its grandeur as we went
inside.

Growing up, I had never thought of myself as poor. Of course, we were living at
Cameron Hall then, and its gracious rooms
were refurbished over a period of time. But
all around were reminders that the South
had been left impoverished in the after-
math of the War. Everyone we knew, in-
cluding most of our immediate family, had
lost everything — not only their menfolk,
but their homes and wealth.

Certainly Uncle Clinton and Aunt Harmony had been similarly affected. It wasn't
until Alair became engaged to Randall
Bondurant that their fortunes changed
dramatically.

We were shown into the elegant parlor
by a uniformed black butler, and I looked

around with unrestrained amazement. Gold-flocked wallpaper, velvet draperies and handsomely carved furniture met my wide-eyed gaze. Over the white marble mantelpiece hung a portrait of Alair that momentarily unnerved me. She looked so alive, smiling that secret smile, head held high, eyes sparkling.

"Well, it appears Harmony and Clint will never want for anything!" Aunt Garnet's voice, tinged with slight sarcasm, snapped me back to the present.

"Yes, and isn't it a blessing, not to have the burden of poverty added to the loss of their only child?"

At Mama's gentle rebuke, Garnet flushed. "Well, of course, money never eased sorrow, but lack of it does cause its own kind of grief. Think of Blythe," she said with a significant inflection.

There was no reply as everyone in the room remembered Uncle Malcolm's widow who had disappeared so mysteriously after Montclair was lost to Bondurant.

Just then Uncle Clinton joined us, followed by the butler bearing a large silver tray with a tea set.

"Harmony isn't quite herself yet," he apologized. "Perhaps later." He wiped his forehead with his handkerchief. "I don't think she'll . . . either of us . . . can ever get over this —"

I heard only fragments of the conversation after that — my mother and aunts offering their words of comfort, Uncle Clint telling his story of the accident that had cost him the life of his adored daughter, the sympathetic responses.

"Her horse was frightened by something, reared — she was thrown —"

"But Alair was an expert horsewoman."

"Unbelievable!"

"Was she alone?"

"Her horse came back with an empty saddle —"

"That beautiful girl —"

"With her whole life ahead of her —"

The last two comments rang a bell. I had heard almost those identical words on Alair's wedding day. Everyone had declared there had never been a more radiant bride. I remembered, too, the look of adoration in Randall's eyes as he watched Alair moving to meet him in the gazebo he especially built for the wedding. At the time I had dreamily wondered if any man would ever look at me like that.

My gaze was drawn once more to the painting of my beautiful cousin. It must have been painted soon after her engagement was announced, for the artist had posed her left hand holding a furled fan to display the large diamond solitaire ring Randall had given her.

I recognized the dress of coral silk with a Spanish flounce of delicate ruffled lace, part of her trousseau, because she had shown off both the dress and her ring to me the same day.

"See, Druscilla," she had said, flashing her finger where the diamond sparkled at me. "Look at this! Some day a handsome prince will come along for you, too, and shower you with jewels and carriages and fine clothes."

Recalling Alair's own prediction and the brevity of her charmed life served only to make me aware of how fleeting are our days, even if they are filled with romance, travel, and wealth.

Randall's face superimposed itself on the portrait before me. The awful transition from his wedding-day happiness to the tragic mask I had seen today wrenched my heart. Too, the faces of the little girls, framed in their black poke bonnets, appeared before me, touching me again with their innocence and vulnerability. What would become of them all?

After Mama, Aunt Garnet, and Auntie

Kate had each spent time in Aunt Harmony's darkened upstairs bedroom, we said our good-byes and drove back to Cameron Hall in silence.

Since Mama and I had plans to leave the next morning to return to Richmond, we retired early. Wearily I removed my simple dark gray dress and sank onto the bed, but I could not dispel my melancholy mood after the depressing events of the day.

"If Jonathan were only here," I murmured. He, more than any other, would have understood what Alair's death meant to me. It was the end of a time when every day had been filled with sunshine.

As children, we three could not have known what our mothers, and in Jonathan's case, Aunt Garnet who took his mother's place after Aunt Rose died in that awful fire, endured. If the grown-ups were worried about the War, their husbands' safety, about providing food or money or clothing for us, we never knew. For us, it was a magical time.

Now reality had ripped away some of that remembered enchantment.

After the War, Jonathan had gone to live with his mother's relatives, his Uncle John and Aunt Frances in Milford, Massachusetts, where the Meredith family were wealthy millowners. It was what Aunt Rose wanted. Shortly before she died, she made Aunt Garnet promise that Jonathan would go to the Merediths if Uncle Malcolm didn't come home from the War. And he hadn't. Not right away, that is. We learned later that he had been captured and held in an enemy prison camp, then had gone West to try to recoup his fortune in the gold fields of California. Eventually, he had come home to Montclair, bringing a new bride, but Jonathan never came to live with them.

I knew Aunt Garnet had sent Jonathan a telegram about Alair's death, but he would not have received the news in time to come to the funeral.

What would he have thought of Randall Bondurant and Alair's two pitiful little girls? The poignant picture of the little family haunted me. I could still see the children in their identical white dresses sashed with black ribbon, their black capes billowing in the wind.

That scene of the bereaved father, the motherless children begged to be committed to paper. I got out the sketch book I always carried with me and began to draw my impressions.

I'm not sure how long I worked at it, but

I was not satisfied with my quick rendition when I finished it. I studied it for a long time, then put it away.

The memory was not so easily laid aside. I lay awake for some time before finally falling into a shallow sleep, troubled with strange dreams and sudden awakenings.

Back in Richmond, I continued my preparations for my first year of teaching. Thornycroft sounded dismal to me, and Massachusetts, a world away. Still, I was cheered by the prospect of a reunion with Jonathan, now a student at Harvard, which was located near the school where I would be teaching.

With the time for my departure approaching, Mama grew pensive, and I found myself consoling her, rather than the other way around.

"You know how much I hate leaving you, Mama," I said, "but the salary Thornycroft pays is more than is paid by any of our Southern academies. And with the money I will be able to save, we'll soon be able to afford a place of our own."

She gave me a wan smile and patted my cheek, but she didn't say any more.

The Sunday before I left for Massachusetts, Mama and I went to church together as usual. It seemed to me that both the text for the sermon, Isaiah 58:11, and the closing hymn had been chosen just for me.

He leadeth me! O blessed tho't!
O words with heavn'ly comfort fraught!
Whate'er I do, where'er I be,
Still, 'tis God's hand that leadeth me!

He leadeth me, He leadeth me,
By His own hand He leadeth me:
His faithful foll'wer I would be,
For by His hand He leadeth me.

I sang the words with complete assurance that they were true.

I was glad I'd been grounded in that kind of truth from an early age. But I had no idea how my faith would be tested in the days ahead.

Mama insisted on coming down to the depot with me to see me off on the train although I begged her not to, knowing how hard it would be to say good-by. As we kissed, hugged for the last time, I said through my tears, "Next year, I'll find a job closer to home, I promise."

Mama's small figure grew smaller and smaller as I looked back from the train window. My last glimpse of her, waving bravely, strengthened my determination to keep that promise.

There was no way I could know that day what unexpected circumstances would make my promise impossible to keep.

chapter
3

The first time I saw Randall Bondurant was at Alair's wedding; the second time, at her funeral. I never expected to see him again.

But once in awhile, I'd come across that sketch I'd made of him and of the two little girls, and I would be reminded of him. I would study the features I had drawn from memory, knowing that I had failed to capture something intrinsic in the expression, something hidden in the eyes, something just beyond my skill to grasp.

The faces of the children had come quite easily. It had been Randall's I kept erasing, resketching, yet never feeling satisfied.

I'd put it away again, wondering why it continued to fascinate me.

To tell the truth, ever since I had been in their wedding, Randall had been a romantic figure in my imagination.

In the sheltered world of my childhood, he had emerged like some hero out of a fairy tale — a darkly handsome prince, dashing, mysterious. He had spoken but a few words to me after the ceremony, but bowed over my hand, kissing my fingertips, and declaring me to be the loveliest bridesmaid in the bridal party. He had been gracious to all the family, charming them in spite of their pride and pre-wedding prejudice.

I realized he had remained in my imagination all these years, fantasy obscuring the reality I had seen that day. I studied my sketch of his ravaged face. Still superimposed upon the penciled lines were the god-like features of my girlish dreams. With a sigh, I gave up and slid the sketch back into my portfolio.

I had little time for such thoughts of the past. There were so many new people, new sights, new experiences surrounding me in my position. My teaching assignments were demanding, my pupils interesting, and my time fully occupied with duties. Although I was very lonely at times, the longer I was at Thornycroft, the farther away Virginia seemed.

The brightest spot in my first winter in New England was Jonathan. The first day he came to see me, he created quite a stir among the female students. This didn't surprise me.

I've always thought Jonathan should be the subject for some great sculpture. He is tall and well built with black curly hair worn rather long, like a poet. His eyes are dark and full of intelligence. But just when you think he may be much too serious to be interesting, a dimple pops out in his left cheek, his eyes twinkle mischievously, and he breaks out in a disarming grin. Dear Jonathan!

We had a glorious time that day, for it was my afternoon off, and we lunched at an elegant hotel where we interrupted each other frequently in our eagerness to catch up on all that had happened in our lives since we had last seen each other. Of course, a main topic of our conversation was Alair's death.

"There's really quite a bit of mystery about that," I told him. "Her horse came back to the stables with the stirrup broken. They found her body later in the woods. Whether she was thrown or somehow fell off and struck her head on a rock, no one knows for sure. But the cause of death was a fatal skull fracture, so they say."

Jonathan shook his head. "I find it hard to believe. Everyone knows that Alair was practically born in the saddle."

"I know. It was a shock to everyone."

There was a lull in the conversation while we finished our lobster bisque.

"How is Auntie Kate?" he asked. I knew he was eager for all the news, since he had chosen to take the Grand Tour of Europe, a gift from his Uncle John, instead of visiting Mayfield the summer before.

"Oh, as dear as ever!" I told him. "She has arthritis, but you never hear her complain. She's up early every morning, working in her beloved garden."

"And your mother?"

"Mama's fine, Jonathan. She's still taking care of Aunt Nell Perry, you know." I paused. "That's one of the reasons I took this job at Thornycroft. The pay is so much better than I could get closer home. I hope one day to be able to support Mama fully . . . so we can have our own home."

"Don't tell me you plan to be a spinster, Dru," he teased. "Surely there's some young man in Virginia pining away for you to come back and marry him."

I blushed. "Not really, Jonathan. I don't have any intentions of marrying until Mama is comfortably settled."

"Unless you find some rich bachelor like

Alair did." Jonathan had barely uttered those words when he halted, looking stricken. "What a stupid thing to say! I'm sorry. It just slipped out."

"I understand," I said, remembering Alair's ambition. "But then we both always knew Alair felt she had to marry money. I think she always loved Brett Tolliver, but he was just as poor as the rest of us."

"Well, it was a terrible thing to say." He seemed genuinely ashamed. Then he asked, "What about her two little girls, her husband? What's happened to them?"

"All I know is what Mama wrote. Shortly after the funeral, Bondurant closed the house and took the children and went away — nobody knows where."

Jonathan changed the subject. "How about Uncle Rod?"

"He wasn't in Mayfield when we were there. Auntie Kate said he had gone to Ireland . . . on a horse-buying trip."

Uncle Rod raised and sold thoroughbreds, and had a profitable business. So profitable was it that Auntie Kate was able to close the school.

I leaned forward and, in a stage whisper, added, "Later I overheard Aunt Garnet say to Mama that she hoped Rod wasn't on another 'wild goose chase' — whatever that means!" I giggled. "Have you ever known a family with so many secrets, Jonathan?"

When we had drawn out our luncheon until we noticed the waiters exchanging disapproving looks, we withdrew reluctantly and walked back to Thornycroft in the brisk sunshine. At the gate, Jonathan promised to come again soon.

"Aunt Frances wants you to come out to the house. They're all anxious to meet you — especially Norvell. But I'll have to warn you about my cousin. He has an eye for pretty girls."

"What about you, Jonathan? Is there anyone special in your life?"

Immediately he colored. "Well . . . yes." He smiled shyly. "You'll meet her when you come out to Milford. Her name is Davida Carpenter. Her father, Kendall Carpenter, used to be in love with my mother. That was before she met and married my father. Small world, isn't it?"

We laughed together and said good-by, Jonathan telling me that Mrs. Meredith would send a written invitation for the weekend after next.

It was too far, too expensive, and the weather too uncertain for me to attempt the long trip to Virginia for Christmas, so at their invitation I spent the holidays with the Merediths.

Their huge, many-gabled house of brown shingle was circled with balconies and verandas. Inside all was homey warmth. Fires crackled cheerfully in every room. Bright curtains hung at the windows and braided rugs splashed color and warmth underfoot. Books crammed ample shelves and spilled over tabletops, and framed landscapes adorned the walls.

It was a lively, happy place to be. Someone always seemed to be playing the piano, opening doors, running up and down the wide staircase.

Presiding over the kitchen was a good-natured Irish cook named Birdie. The downstairs maid, Violet, and an upstairs maid called Polly kept everything in order, with a minimum of direction from the efficient Frances Meredith. Looking on with amused tolerance was Jonathan's Uncle John.

The whole ten days of my visit, the house was filled with young people — Norvie's and Jonathan's classmates from Harvard and Norvie's sister Ellen's girlfriends from Milford's Day Academy.

I discovered to my surprise that Northerners could be as gracious and hospitable as Southerners.

I roomed with Ellen who was a delightful chatterbox. I think she had a hopeless crush on Jonathan, but true to his word, he proved to be devoted to the quiet, but very lovely Davida Carpenter.

There were taffy-pulls and popcorn parties, games of Charades and Quotes, square dances and round robin suppers, where we went from house to house for each different course.

I learned to ice skate on the frozen pond behind the house, often with the roguish Norvie as my partner. Jonathan was right; his cousin was a polished charmer. Forewarned, I took all his compliments with the proverbial grain of salt.

Two days before Christmas, we all went into the woods to select a tree. After cutting it down, we dragged it home and decorated it with yards of popped corn and cranberries draped over its fragrant cedar boughs. Then we hung cornucopias filled with candies, paper rings, tinsel stars, and painted angels with gilt wings. Finally, when the tree was abloom with its borrowed finery, we topped it with a perfect gold star.

Gathering around the spinet, we sang familiar carols until the silent night vibrated with our joyous welcome to the Christ child. One by one, we found a comfortable spot near the fire and, sipping mugs of spiced cider, brought the evening to a peaceful close with stories of childhood Christmases past.

Christmas Eve was the loveliest of all. We attended the Midnight Candlelight Service in the steepled, white frame church in the village, then walked home across the snow-clad roads that glistened in the cold moonlight to open presents and feast on fruitcake and punch. Finally, we tumbled exhausted, into our beds as the first gray light of dawn was peeping over the hills.

Mama's Christmas present to me had arrived before I left Thornycroft. I opened the package with great anticipation, knowing Mama always made me something very special. I pushed aside the tissue paper eagerly and lifted out a beautiful, green taffeta dress. It rustled and shimmered as I shook it out, then held it up against myself and looked in the mirror. The color was perfect, making my chameleon blue-green eyes shine like emeralds. It was fashioned in the newest French style with an over-skirt drawn back, fluted flounces rippling down the back, and corded braid trim in a darker green velvet. I knew Mama, an expert seamstress, must have copied it from one of the Parisian fashion plates published in her pattern books.

I wore it the night of the New Year's Eve party to the envious sighs of Ellen, the approving nod of Aunt Frances, and Norvie's admiring smile.

I think, for the first time in my life, I felt really attractive. I had always compared my looks to Alair's Dresden beauty. I had grown up thinking myself too tall and thin, my thick dark hair too heavy to curl in contrast to Alair's blond ringlets.

But that night my dance card was filled, and the in-between sets vied for by several young Harvard men. I basked, at least temporarily, in the fleeting popularity of a "belle."

At midnight I found myself under the mistletoe with Norvie, who much to my astonishment, gave me my first "non-kin" kiss.

Then we all clustered around the Prophecy cake Aunt Frances had baked, waiting for the favors we might find in our slice that might foretell what the new year held for us. A tiny metal ship meant a sea voyage; a shiny penny meant an inheritance or fortune, and so on. When I found a wedding ring, I was immediately the target for all kinds of teasing conjecture.

I looked over at Jonathan, wondering if he remembered my declaration that I had no intention of marrying until I had secured my mother's comfort. But Jonathan had eyes only for Davida — a slim, pretty girl with fly-away brown hair and laughing gray eyes.

I enjoyed my holiday with the Merediths so much that returning to Thornycroft proved overwhelmingly depressing.

I had already found faculty life unduly restrictive for someone of my artistic temperament. With no outside contacts except the girls' parents and no person of my own age among my colleagues, I sometimes felt that, if I stayed there, I might wither inside, grow older, crankier, and more eccentric every year. And if the routine and rules were hard for the girls, the expectations for the teachers, as required by Headmistress Amelia Pitts, were impossible. I lived for my freedom on Thursday afternoons.

That is why on this particular Thursday — a windblown, blue day in mid-March — I was filled with a restless desire to escape. I packed a reed basket with a sketch pad, my small box of watercolors, a piece of plum cake, and an apple from the kitchen.

As free as any child playing hooky, I sprinted through the orchard behind the school, took the path through the woods, and crossed the curved stone bridge to the park. I found myself an empty bench near the children's playground on which to eat my picnic.

From there, I had a view of the lake, where black swans glided, and of the graceful willows just beginning to green. I could see the swings and slides, where the uniformed nannies from the great houses fronting the Commons brought their charges later in the afternoon.

I had been sketching happily for perhaps an hour when I looked up from my pad and spotted the two little girls. It may have been their outfits that caught my attention — purple velvet caped coats and bonnets, fur-trimmed and beribboned and much too fussy for playing freely on this spring-like afternoon. Or maybe it was the dour-faced woman in black sitting on the bench opposite the swings. She seemed forever to be barking directions, corrections, and admonitions.

Oh, why doesn't she let them alone! I thought to myself. *Let them enjoy themselves!*

In spite of the continual harping of the sharp-featured woman with her sour expression, the two little girls seemed to take delight in each other, and the sound of their pure laughter warmed my heart. Suddenly I longed to capture the essence of this moment of innocent happiness.

I tore off the sketch I was working on and started a new one. I worked swiftly and with inspiration, my pen and then my brush moving with light washes, hoping to catch the magic of the scene.

As the nurse continued to scold, I saw all the joy drain from the two rosy little faces and I felt a rush of anger at the woman's insensitivity. As soon as her back was turned, however, they dimpled mischievously and resumed their play.

Good! I thought, identifying with the small rebellion.

Sketching in the two small figures, the taller one so sweetly protective as she helped her little sister into the swing and gently pushed her, I saw almost at once that the children transformed my rather ordinary landscape into a charming scene.

Just then a long shadow fell across the picture.

"That's very good."

The deep masculine voice so startled me

41

that I knocked over my tin cup of water, making a clumsy grab and almost upsetting my sketchpad in the process.

"Sorry. I didn't mean to frighten you. But those are my children you're painting —"

The sun was at my back so that I had to shield my eyes with one hand as I twisted half-way round to look up at the speaker.

As I did so, a shock of recognition momentarily stunned me. This man was no stranger. His was the face I'd seen in a hundred dreams, the face that had haunted me for a long time — ever since Alair's funeral.

The face I was staring into was that of my cousin's widower — Randall Bondurant.

chapter
4

Randall Bondurant! What was he doing here in Boston? And under what extraordinary set of circumstances should we meet after all this time?

As I struggled to find my voice, he continued to study me intently, drawing his straight dark brows together over piercing eyes.

He seemed thinner, his face a little sterner. New lines etched on either side of his mouth made his features appear sharper. He had removed his hat, and I noticed that his thick, dark hair was finely threaded with silver.

He was splendidly dressed in a gray, velvet-collared greatcoat, a silk scarf at his throat, gray suede gloves. I noticed the black mourning band on his sleeve.

I had remained silent, undecided as to whether I should admit knowing him when he spoke again.

"Your painting is really very nice. And

since those children are my daughters, I would like to purchase it, if I may."

Still, I hesitated.

"The picture," he repeated somewhat impatiently. "May I buy it?"

While I sat mute, something curious flickered in his eyes. "Is something wrong?" he demanded. "Do I know you?"

I got to my feet then, swallowed over my suddenly dry throat, and replied, "We've met. I'm Druscilla Montrose, Alair's cousin."

I watched his eyes widen in disbelief, then narrow appraisingly. "But there is no resemblance. None! There should at least be a family resemblance, shouldn't there?"

I knew he was comparing my dark hair and vivid coloring with Alair's delicate fairness, and the color in my cheeks heightened perceptibly.

"Perhaps," I murmured. "I take more after the Montrose side of the family, I think."

"Druscilla." He repeated my name as if trying to remember. Then his countenance brightened. "*Little* Dru! The youngest bridesmaid. The one Alair had to fight to have in the wedding. But you were just a child then." Sweeping my form from head to toe, he shook his head. "You're hardly a child anymore though, are you?"

Again I felt my face grow warm under his assessing gaze. I turned to look toward the swings where the nurse seemed to be fussing again.

"The little girls —" I began.

"Yes. My daughters, Lenora and Lalage, We call them Nora and Lally." He bit his lip as if remembering belatedly that there was no longer a "we." "Come. Let me introduce you." He led the way to the play area.

"Well, my dears," he said, "I have a surprise for you. Say hello to your cousin from Virginia — Druscilla Montrose." Then he bowed stiffly to the nurse. "Miss Ogilvie, the children's nurse."

I offered my hand which she ignored, merely nodding with an expression that looked as if she had just tasted a lemon.

The little girls smiled steadily at me — their hair, their coloring, their demeanor so like Alair that it nearly took my breath away.

Randall then spoke to the nurse, whose mouth was pinched into a straight line in her gray pudding face. "It's getting quite cold. Perhaps you'd best take the children back to the hotel to have their tea. I shall be along presently."

At his dismissal, she gave a little toss of her head, but in a saccharine voice said to the girls, "Come along, young ladies, let's go have a nice tea."

I felt the sweet tone rang false, for they seemed to take leave rather reluctantly. As they turned and started away I saw, over Bondurant's shoulder, how she jerked the arm of the youngest child and gave the older one an impatient push. My impulse was to call this behavior to their father's attention, but he snapped a question that demanded my answer.

"What are you doing so far from home?"

I explained my situation briefly. The wind off the lake was becoming chill, and I shivered and began gathering my things. "I must get back. I head a table at supper, and supervise an evening study hall."

He held up my painting. "Then, may I have this?"

"Oh, yes!" I was secretly flattered.

"And you're sure you won't accept payment?"

"Oh, no!" I said emphatically.

"Very well then. Thank you, Miss Montrose." He made a slight bow, tipping his hat and replacing it. Then he turned and, without a backward glance, moved at a brisk pace down the path.

As I hurried back to Thornycroft through the gathering winter dusk, I could not help wondering at this unexpected encounter with Randall Bondurant and his two little girls. What darlings! They deserved better than that grim, unsmiling warden of a governess . . . or whatever she was! I shook off the disagreeable feeling. But, for the life of me, during the next few weeks, I could not altogether halt the invasion of these three into my thoughts and dreams.

I sat at the slant-top teacher's desk in the third form classroom one afternoon, doggedly correcting English test papers, too occupied with the work at hand to think of that unique meeting four weeks prior. Outside, an April rain fell steadily. The sky was dreary and gray and heavy with clouds promising more rain to soak the already sodden ground.

It had been cold all month, and even the trees I could see from the long narrow windows were still bare, devoid of anything but the most primitive of buds to forecast a long-delayed spring. I shivered and chafed my arms to encourage the circulation, casting a baleful eye at the small corner stove with its meager supply of coal. No prisoner behind bars could have felt more confined at that moment!

Suddenly the door opened, and a bright-eyed student, her head topped with coppery curls, popped in. "Miss Ames said for me to tell you you have a visitor in the parlor, Miss Montrose."

A visitor? I frowned and deposited my pen in the inkwell. But I never had visitors. I knew no one in the area . . . except the Merediths in Milford. I jumped to my feet, accidentally sending some of the papers sailing off into the air. *Jonathan!* I thought, with a surge of joy. Of course! It must be Jonathan!

I rushed out the door and flew down the three flights of steps, managing to slow my steps to a more sedate pace as I approached the corridor where the study hall door stood open. I felt the curious stares of the students as I passed.

Throwing open the parlor door, I had formed Jonathan's name on my lips when I realized that the tall man standing before me was not my cousin, after all. Quickly, I remembered my manners.

"Good afternoon, Mr. Bondurant."

He nodded, bowing slightly, and greeted me solemnly. "Miss Montrose."

"Won't you be seated?" I gestured to the

high-back horsehair sofa, then took the straight chair opposite him.

He looked even sterner and more forbidding than at our meeting in the park weeks ago. His high cheekbones, the prominent jawline, and the reddish cast of his skin gave him the appearance of an Indian, despite his expensively tailored suit. His cravat was black as was the mourning band encircling his arm.

"First of all," he began, "I apologize for not having contacted you sooner, nor following up on my suggestion that I arrange a time when you and your cousins could get acquainted. Unforeseen circumstances prevented . . . the most pressing being that both little girls have been ill." At my expression of concern, he hurried on, "Oh, not serious illness, mind you, just heavy colds. Still, their recovery has been slow. I fear this New England climate is too harsh for them." He paused significantly, and I waited.

"In a few days we will be leaving for Virginia," he said, slanting me a look I could not quite discern.

The stab of disappointment I felt at his words registered painfully, startling me with its intensity. After all, I didn't even know the little girls, I could hardly miss them, could I? And yet I had a distinct feeling of loss. It must have shown in my expression, for I have one of those tell-tale faces where emotion cannot hide.

Randall held up his hand as if to check my response. "I have come here today . . . presumed to take you from your duties . . . to make a proposal. I trust you will consider it in much less time than it has taken me to undertake the request." He smiled sardonically, and I waited in exquisite tension, wondering what kind of "proposal" he might have in mind.

"I would like you to accept the position of my children's governess . . . companion." He paused while the gravity of those words sank into my consciousness. I was too stunned for comment and he went on. "Needless to say, it has been very difficult finding a suitable person to fill . . . to step into such an important place in the lives of my children. I have found Miss Ogilvie entirely . . . well, let us just say that I made a hasty and regrettable choice in hiring her at the suggestion of a very respected person whose judgment I trusted perhaps too readily, a Mrs. Elliot of a fine Boston family. However, that is neither here nor there —" He stepped over to the window and looked out into the drizzly day. I suspected he was not seeing anything at all, merely politely putting some distance between us in order for me to take in this strange new idea.

"I will pay a generous salary, and you will have ample time to spend as you like, perhaps with your relatives . . . who, after all, are my children's relatives too." At that, he turned to eye me warily, as if testing me for my reaction. "They should know their mother's family better. . . . And, if I'm not mistaken, I rather thought you might enjoy returning to Virginia yourself. At any rate, I would be pleased if you would give this matter your earliest consideration . . . perhaps even as early as tomorrow afternoon, which, I believe is your day off."

I nodded. The man knew everything! I had to give him credit for his research, but words still failed to come.

"Then," he continued, taking up the gloves he had flung across the back of a chair, "the children and I would be pleased if you would join us for tea. I shall send a carriage . . . shall we say three o'clock?"

Throughout the long recital, I had remained silent, while my thoughts rambled. He must think me a perfect idiot! Now I rose to my feet with as much dignity as I could muster. "I really don't know what to say, Mr. Bondurant. Tea is one thing, of course, but accepting such a position —"

He waved aside my attempted protest with an impatient gesture. "Oh, I'm not asking for an immediate answer. You'll have some time to think." He strode purposefully to the door where he turned, his hand resting on the doorknob. "Until tomorrow then?"

When Bondurant had gone I sat down, my knees suddenly quite unsteady. What a turn of events! Then I remembered I had planned to meet Jonathan on Thursday. I would have to get word to him. His reaction to all this was important to me, and I found myself eager to tell him.

The Bondurant suite into which I was shown was luxurious and ornate in the extreme, but in excellent taste, for the hotel was one of the city's finest and most prestigious. Heavy dark velvet draperies swagged the long windows, and tufted velvet sofas and chairs rested on a handsome Oriental rug.

Randall rose from behind a massive mahogany desk to greet me and I noticed at once that the children's governess, the gaunt-faced woman I'd seen with them in the park, was seated in a high-backed chair nearby.

"Ah, Miss Montrose, right on time. I admire promptness. You remember Miss Ogilvie, the children's nurse, don't you?" Randall asked smoothly.

The woman regarded me with an icy stare as I took my seat.

"I have asked you here to discuss my daughters' future education," Randall continued. "I felt it would be both helpful and informative, perhaps mutually beneficial, for you both to contribute to what I hope will be an open and friendly interchange of ideas."

I looked at Miss Ogilvie, gave her a tentative smile, and received in return a look of outright hostility. It was clear that she considered me the "enemy."

It did not take Randall long to get to the point.

"Well, Miss Ogilvie, I foresee making some changes, notably some extensive travel with my children, with frequent and perhaps sudden changes of residence. You see, I am interested in finding a new permanent home for my family and business interests. This would, I fear, cause some disruption in the kind of stable routine you're accustomed to. What I'm looking for, I suppose, is a less rigid way of life for my daughters, one that will permit more flexibility."

"I have been governess in some of the finest homes in New England, with some of the best families of Boston . . ." She drew herself up to her complete height, which was considerable. To anyone less imperturbable than Mr. Bondurant, she would have appeared quite formidable.

But Randall merely shrugged. "But these are little southern girls, Miss Ogilvie — Virginians. They are used to a gentler life, a more affectionate manner."

"I believe in discipline, Mr. Bondurant. I believe in instilling early the rules of conduct that will stay with a young person throughout life. Children need a firm hand. They mustn't be allowed to —"

"Yes, yes, Miss Ogilvie, I know your convictions," Randall interrupted, "and I respect your right to hold them. But for my daughters, I have decided on a less strict method of rearing them. Frankly, I am not of the persuasion that 'sparing the rod spoils the child.' I hold the opposite view, in fact. I believe harsh measures embitter and destroy the spirit of a child." Randall's mouth tightened visibly and I could not help wondering if he were speaking from his own experience.

"So you see we have a grave difference of opinion in this matter, and that is why I fear . . . no, not fear, *regret* for your sake, Miss Ogilvie, that I have come to the conclusion that you are not the proper person to be in charge of my daughters. You will, of course, receive a month's salary in lieu of notice."

So casual and relaxed was Randall's manner that I was unprepared for Miss Ogilvie's explosive reaction. "Does this mean, sir, that you are dismissing me?"

"Relieving you would be the better term, my dear lady. Miss Montrose, the children's cousin, has consented to assume the position of . . . more than governess . . . to my daughters." At this, I could not suppress a sharp intake of breath. "She will know how my . . . wife . . . would have wished them to be brought up. And now, if you will be so kind —"

Randall pulled the tapestry bell cord, indicating that the consultation, if that's what it was, had ended. "As you know, I had a previous engagement and so I must conclude our discussion."

Taking this as my cue, also, I stood and so did Miss Ogilvie. She cast a scathing look in my direction, then holding herself haughtily erect, swept from the room.

I put on my gloves hurriedly and moved toward the door.

"Wait," said Bondurant softly. He cocked his head, listening as the double doors clicked sharply behind Miss Ogilvie, who was making her departure with evident displeasure.

Randall turned to me with a smile that transformed his serious expression. "Now, we can breathe a sigh of relief. An unpleasant chore out of the way. A chance to relax and speak of much pleasanter things —"

"But I thought you said you had a previous engagement."

"But I do. Don't you recall I asked you to have tea with us?"

In the drama of the last half-hour, that invitation had completely slipped my mind. All I could concentrate on was the bizarre encounter with Miss Ogilvie and Randall's explanation for her dismissal. Extensive travel? Frequent changes of residence? Presumably, where he and the children went, the governess was sure to go. The endless possibilities dazzled my imagination.

Randall's reminder of our pre-arranged "tea party" with the little girls brought me quickly back to the present.

"I hope I did not overstep the bounds of propriety by telling Miss Ogilivie you had accepted the offer, did I?" Randall looked at me inquiringly. "I assumed you had, or else you would not have come in person. You would have sent a note of refusal. Am I right?" His face was serious, but I thought I discerned a glimmer of amusement in his eyes.

"Yes, of course. I — I mean, yes, I find that I do want to accept the position, after all," I stammered. I was annoyed with myself for feeling flustered under his steady gaze.

Thankfully, there was a knock at the door and a maid in a black dress and starched ruffled apron and cap entered with my two little cousins.

"You asked that I bring the children at four, sir," she said to Randall, bobbing a small curtsy.

"Fine! Come in, girls!" Randall smiled and held out his arms, and they both came running to him. "Say hello to your cousin Druscilla."

From the safety of his embrace, they peeked out at me. They both had a little trouble with my name, especially Lally, who had a tiny lisp. But in no time at all, we gathered around the sumptuous tea table that was brought up by one of the hotel staff and were chatting easily.

Both children seemed very bright and, although a little shy with me that day, I never had a moment's doubt that I would love my little cousins and that they, in turn, would love me.

Before I left that day, Randall and I made the arrangements for assuming the position as the children's governess. He and the children would remain in Boston until he had concluded his business, then return to Virginia; I would follow the last week in May, at the end of the school term at Thornycroft. In the meantime, Randall suggested that I plan to spend my days off with Lenora and Lalage so that we could get to know each other better before I took over their care officially.

On the way down to call a carriage to take me back to school, he said, "I hope you won't regret your decision."

"Why should I?" I asked, thinking that the enormous raise in pay and the opportunity to be near Mama again, not to mention being with his delightful children, seemed more a windfall than any cause for regret.

"Things are not always as they seem," he

remarked enigmatically. "But then you are still very young. Life has not played many tricks on you yet."

There was no time to reply, for the carriage had come and he handed me courteously into it.

I drove away, thinking that in one way at least, he was right. I'd never seen such a twist and turn of fate as meeting him again, becoming his children's governess! But I could not then see any reason to regret it.

chapter
5

From childhood I had been taught to pray before making any decision. But how often do we seek God's blessing on what we have already decided to do?

Even Mama's cautionary reply when I wrote to her of Randall's offer and my plans to accept it did nothing to dampen my own enthusiasm for the opportunity. Even Jonathan's more direct question — "Do you really think it's a good idea?" — did not deter me.

I knew there would be the predictable clucking among the aunts about the wisdom of my taking such a position. Everyone had assumed that, upon Alair's death, Randall Bondurant need no longer be considered, even remotely, a part of the family.

But I didn't care what people said. I had had enough of Thornycroft with its gaunt, gray halls, its strict regimen, its drafty classrooms, its indifferent students and aloof faculty. Nor would I miss the cold porridge and lukewarm coffee served for breakfast, the stiff Parents' Day teas, and the unrelenting "code of conduct" for teachers, imposed by the formidable head-mistress.

At the end of the term, I left Thorny-croft without a backward glance and boarded the train for Virginia with happy anticipation and high hopes.

The week I spent in Richmond with Mama at Aunt Nell's was a busy one. There were duty calls to make on some rel-atives, and visits from others, curious about my decision. Mama was a great help to me during these episodes, tactfully steering the conversation so that I, in-censed by all the unasked-for advice, did not offend anyone with sharp retorts. Actually, I did not think it was anyone else's business. The money Randall was paying me far exceeded any inner doubts of my own about accepting the position.

We were also occupied with my ward-robe, eliminating the heavy winter things I'd needed up North and substituting those I would need for the hot Virginia summer. Mama surprised me with two pretty new dresses she had made for me.

But with all the visits, the fittings, the whirl of activity, we had little time alone. It was only the night before I was to leave for Mayfield that we had a chance for a real talk.

Mama came into my bedroom as I was putting the last items into my trunk. "Are you all ready then?" she asked, a wistful note creeping into her voice.

"Yes, just about," I replied. Seeing the pensive expression on her face, I gave her a fierce hug. "Don't look so sad, Mama. I'm only going a few miles away this time. It's not the same as when I left for Thornycroft."

She held me close. "I know, dear. It's just that —"

I drew back, looked into her eyes. "Just what?"

"You're stepping into such a different world — one that changed Alair, took her away from her family —"

"But Mama, I'm not *marrying* Randall Bondurant!" I protested. "I'm simply going to work for him."

Mama patted my cheek. "Of course, dear."

"And I'll be near enough to visit often. Maybe I can bring the little girls. Oh, Mama, you'll love them! They look so much like Alair and they're so sweet —" I rattled on, hoping to banish that sad look from her eyes. Or was I trying to quiet any last-minute doubts of my own?

"Come, let me brush your hair like I did when you were a child," Mama said, picking up the hairbrush.

So I sat on a low stool in front of her while she rhythmically stroked the brush through my long hair until my scalp tingled and I grew pleasantly drowsy.

"There now," she said at last. "Come, I'll even tuck you in like the old days."

As she leaned down to kiss me good night, I reached up and put my arms around her. "Please don't worry about me, Mama. Everything's going to be fine."

"I hope so, darling," she said, then added gently, "Don't ever forget, Dru, who you are and what your values are. Remember . . . all the money in the world, all the luxuries, don't necessarily bring happiness. They didn't in Alair's case —" she broke off and then quickly went on, "Taking care of those children will be a heavy responsibility. Pray for guidance and read your Bible every day."

"I will, Mama," I promised, seeing the concern in her eyes.

"Sleep well, then, and God bless." She went out of the room, carrying the lamp with her.

Lying in the darkness, waiting for sleep, I wondered why my mother had felt it necessary to give me even gentle warnings. It was as if she feared some unknown danger in my future.

I had not missed the subtle reservations, the ill-concealed misgivings of some of my relatives when they learned of the position I was taking. But I thought Mama understood my reasons, approved my motives. But then, did I really understand them myself?

Before I could answer that question truthfully, I drifted off to sleep.

I stepped off the train at the small, yellow frame station in Mayfield into glorious June sunshine. It was far different from the day, nearly a year ago, when I'd come for Alair's funeral.

"Miss Montrose?" I turned at the sound of my name to see a black man in fine livery smiling in welcome. He took off his square-crowned hat, revealing a grizzled gray head. "I'm from 'Bon Chance,' miss. Mr. Bondurant done sent me to fetch you."

"Thank you," I replied, thinking there was something vaguely familiar about the man. "There is my trunk — that small red one — and my bonnet-box."

He led the way to a handsome open carriage, assisted me in and placed my hatbox carefully on the seat, then buckled on my trunk. Then he swung into his place beside me and picked up the buggy whip.

Before flicking it at the backs of the two chestnut horses, he turned around. A wide grin split his dark face.

"Reckon you doan 'member me, miss. You wuz jest a li'l bit of a thing when you and yo' Mama left Montclair. I'm Trice, miss. Susie's boy. I helped hide de horses when dem Yankees done come."

I had shadowy memories of the terrible time we had all been huddled upstairs when the Union soldiers ransacked the house. It had all been mad confusion — noise, shouts, the sound of booted feet tramping my grandmother's Aubusson rugs. We children had watched it all in wide-eyed horror.

"Well, you can't completely forget things like that," I told him. "I'm glad to see you again, Trice."

"And I'm glad to see you, miss, all growed-up to a pretty young lady. I hear tell you's comin' to live at Montclair again, take care of Miss Alair's chillen."

"That's right."

"Dat's good news. De best we's had in a while. Been sorrowful times, fo' shure!" Trice shook his head then turned, clicked his tongue, and gave a smart slap to the pair.

As we trotted along the pleasant, shaded streets, quiet now in the mid-afternoon of this early summer day, I eagerly looked right and left for familiar landmarks.

The town had changed. The people on the streets were well-dressed; the businesses in the downtown section, thriving; the streets, paved; the houses we passed, freshly painted.

When I was growing up, Mayfield was full of widows and crippled soldiers. Not one home or family had been left untouched by the War. My memory is peopled with veterans with empty sleeves, or leaning on canes, or bundled in rugs, sitting in wheelchairs.

The South seemed to be slowly recovering from its long ordeal — like an invalid gradually beginning to come alive again.

At the edge of town, we paused, then turned onto the wider country road leading out to the large plantations on their sweeping acres.

When we passed the tall wrought-iron gates of Cameron Hall, I knew it wouldn't be long until we'd be approaching Montclair. My pulse quickened in anticipation.

I leaned forward as the carriage rounded the last curve, and I glimpsed the house through the foliage beyond the beautifully kept lawns. The deep woods where I had played with my cousins was on the right; the river, on the left.

I could still feel the cool mossy ground so familiar to my child's bare feet as I looked at the sloping bank, and wiggled my toes, now tightly encased in my grown-up boots. Who would have ever imagined in those days that I would be returning to Montclair as governess to my cousin's children?

I thought again of Alair's funeral and how shocked Aunt Garnet had been that the family had not been received at Montclair, of how Randall, in his grief, had barricaded himself inside, refusing to see anyone. So I had not seen the interior of the house since I had left it many years before.

Montclair, as we had left it — crumbling plaster, faded curtains, ravaged furniture — had been typical of many of the great houses after the War. But even my mother's vivid recollections of the Montrose mansion in the "old days" before the War had not prepared me for what greeted my eyes as the carriage rolled around the circular drive and pulled to a stop in front of the columned porch.

"Montclair"! I breathed the magic name. "Bon Chance" seemed so oddly inappropriate, considering the tragedy that shrouded the place.

I could not conquer a certain sense of melancholy as I mounted the steps. Could a house really renounce its history? Would not the past always be a persistent whisper? Once, the sound of music and laughter echoed through its great halls. Then came the War, with its accompanying toll of death and suffering, filling it with haunting memories. I recalled my mother's sad telling of the disintegration of Malcolm Montrose, heir to Montclair, when he returned after the War, losing himself in bouts of drinking and gambling, until finally, Montclair passed into Bondurant's hands on the turn of a card.

Once again, tragedy had struck, and there was an air of oppressive sadness that was almost palpable the instant I stepped across the threshold.

Inside, I found that much had changed. I looked around the circular center hall, noticing that all the crystal prisms of the great chandelier had been replaced. One by one, the precious hand-cut pieces had been stolen during the Yankee raids. Other changes immediately met my eye: The lovely wainscoting had been painted, and the floor and steps of the curving staircase, once polished to a mellow sheen by a house servant, was now covered with a moss-green, velvety carpeting.

The double doors of the parlor were standing open. From where I stood, I could see that the parlor had been entirely redecorated. Carved furniture, upholstered in satin, replaced the delicate Sheraton tables and the crewel-embroidered, linen-covered wing chairs. Velvet draperies covered the windows and glass-globed lamps topped ornate tables. Over the fireplace hung a large, gold-framed mirror instead of the family portraits I recalled.

The white walls, dark woodwork, and the massive furniture, set upon the lavish floral carpeting, in red, blue, beige and violet, imparted a sense of sumptuousness quite different from the elegant, more refined Montclair I remembered. Perhaps Alair, brought up in the patched shabbiness of the post-War houses we all lived in, wanted the most extravagant and colorful surroundings she could buy.

This house meant many things to me, and I was somewhat dismayed by the changes. As I looked about, I could not help missing the more spacious feeling of the former days. This was not the Montclair where I grew up, but Bondurant's "Bon-Chance."

chapter 6

I'm not sure how long I stood there, wrapped in reverie, until a soft voice drew my attention back to the present.

Standing at the foot of the staircase was a tall, striking-looking woman in a gray poplin dress with a wide, white collar and a starched apron and cap. Dark eyes, set in a coffee-colored face, studied me warily.

"Afternoon, miss," she said. "I'm Vinny. I'm to show you to your room and help you get settled."

"Well, thank you, Vinny."

I turned to see Trice bringing in my trunk and hatbox. "One of de house servants will carry dese upstairs for you, miss," he told me. Then, before he went back outside, he grinned. "Sho' is good to see you back at Montclair — I mean *Bon Chance*." He chuckled. "I keeps forgettin'."

So do I, I thought. *So do I.*

As I started up the broad circular stairway, my hand resting lightly on the polished banister, I caught fragments of the past as they passed quickly through my mind. I imagined how many feet had trod these same steps . . . from the strong woman who had been mistress here in Colonial times to the last bride, Alair! All had come and gone and yet the house, call it what you may, had survived them all and would remain forever "Montclair."

It had stood through Indian raids, fires, and clashes of neighbors on opposite sides of two wars — the War for Independence and the War Between the States, or "The War of Northern Aggression," as I was taught to call it.

Yes, this house had endured both national and personal tragedies and it would go on, whatever happened.

"Come this way, miss." Vinny picked up my hatbox and started up the stairs.

I followed her, pausing before the gallery of the Brides of Montclair. Each young woman who had married a Montrose had been preserved in oil, her portrait commissioned by a world-renowned artist. When she had married Lee Montrose, Mama had followed the tradition, but I didn't remember ever having seen her picture. I wanted to see it now.

I stopped in front of the stunning likeness of a young woman and gazed at it lovingly. Before my father was killed in the War, Mama's hair had been a lustrous sable brown. But it had turned snowy white overnight with the shock of his death.

Slowly I moved on to stand before each portrait of the other brides.

At the landing, I halted. Something was missing.

"Where is the portrait of the children's mother, Miss Alair?" I asked.

Vinny did not turn around right away, but I noticed a stiffening of her shoulders, a certain rigidity as she straightened her back.

"Vinny?" I persisted. "Mama said she was wearing her wedding gown. Randall . . . Mr. Bondurant . . . commissioned it before they were married, said no one was to see it before the wedding. But Aunt Harmony sent for Aunt Garnet and Mama to come see it before it was sent away to be framed. I understand it was life-size. Wasn't it ever hung?"

When Vinny turned around, I was startled at the change in her expression. The full mouth had tightened into a straight line; the huge dark eyes blazed with anger.

"Yes'm, it was. Right on the landin' of

the staircase, so's you could see it from downstairs and as you was comin' up. Miss Alair look jest like an angel in that picture. But Mr. Randall . . . he had it taken down the day she died. Had Trice take it up to the attic. But I don't think that was right, ma'am. She the children's mother, no matter what. No ma'am. Not right." She shook her head.

I was taken aback by the trembling fury in her voice, the wild look in her eyes, the way her hands were balled into tight fists at her side.

"But why would he do that . . . unless in his sorrow he couldn't bear to be reminded of his loss?" I mused aloud.

In our family, it was considered more proper to hang portraits of dead relatives than of living ones. Usually, these were draped with crepe, and often enclosed within the frame were pressed flowers from the casket or perhaps even a lock of hair. Southerners always mourned their dead openly and with great ceremony. That's why the missing portrait was so disturbing.

"No ma'am, I doan think —" She stopped mid-sentence, her eyes widening before she ducked quickly and scurried up the rest of the steps. I was left alone, puzzled for only a moment by her sudden de-

74

parture, for just then I heard a voice behind me.

"I trust your journey was not too tiring, nor the trip from Richmond too uncomfortable."

I whirled around, grabbing hold of the banister to steady myself, and faced my employer, my dead cousin's husband. He stared at me without expression.

"Not at all," I murmured, wondering how much of the conversation with Vinny he had overheard.

"The girls have been waiting impatiently for you all afternoon. They've been most anxious to see you. Perhaps after you've refreshed yourself, Vinny could take you to them," he said. Then, projecting his voice authoritatively in the direction of Vinny's flight, he asked, "Are Miss Lenora and Miss Lalage in the nursery wing?"

"Yes, sir, Mr. Randall," she called from her hiding place. "Matty tried to get them to take a rest before Miss Dru arrived, but I doan know for sure if they did," Vinny answered primly.

"Well, after you help Miss Montrose get settled, see about it."

"Yes sir."

"I hope everything will be satisfactory," he said to me. "I didn't know which room was yours when you lived here as a child, but I have ordered the rooms overlooking the gardens to be readied for you . . . unless you have some preference —" Randall's face was masked behind the brooding eyes.

"I'm sure everything will be fine," I replied, still wondering if he had heard my questions to Vinny.

"Then I shall leave you to get settled. I'll be dining out this evening, so you will have dinner alone with the children. It will give you a chance to get to know them better."

With that, he gave me a curt nod, turned, and walked back into one of the downstairs rooms, shutting the door behind him.

When Vinny reappeared, her subdued manner revealed that the Master of Bon Chance was one whose word was law, and she intended to abide by it. There was no idle chatter as she led me to the room that had been prepared for me.

It was luxurious beyond my imagining — spacious and beautifully appointed. The furniture was French, of pale wood. Everything else was blue and white — the scrolled wallpaper, the blue draperies and white lace curtains adorning the windows that opened onto a balcony with a view of the river in the distance. Off the bedroom was a small sitting room with a fireplace of white marble, a daintily curved sofa upholstered in blue satin, a desk, and two armchairs.

"As soon as I've freshened up, Vinny, I'd like to see the children."

"Yes, ma'am. I'll be back shortly." Vinny left the room quickly, obviously relieved to be gone. Maybe she felt she had talked too much.

I poured water from the china pitcher into the porcelain washbowl decorated with morning glories. Lathering with the fragrant English lavender soap bar, I washed away the dusty feel of my train trip and the ride along country roads.

I changed from my traveling dress into something lighter and was just pinning up my hair again when Vinny's light knock sounded at the door.

She led the way down the hall from my suite, stopping in front of a closed white paneled door and holding her finger up to her lips. There was a suggestion of laughter in her eyes. From behind the door we heard suppressed giggles. Slowly, the door opened — at first, just a crack, then a little wider.

Two curly blond heads, one just a bit

higher than the other, two rosy little faces, two pairs of large dark eyes, looked out at us. There was a minute's hesitation, then the door was pushed back and two flying figures dashed out and flung themselves at me. I bent down and gathered Alair's little daughters into my arms, kissing their sweet-smelling cheeks, the tops of their tangled curls. I felt a lump welling up in my throat. I loved them already, I thought, not knowing then how very dear they would become to me and how irrevocably, from this moment on, our lives would be entwined.

The little girls had had their baths and were in frilled nighties and matching pink robes. But their eyes were bright and alert, with not a hint of sleepiness.

Off their bedroom, with the twin canopied beds, was a large combination school and playroom. It was there at a low, round table set in a bay window overlooking the garden, that supper was set.

"Do you ask a blessing?" I asked them as we seated ourselves.

Both little faces looked blank. With a sinking heart, I realized that these two small souls must have had no religious training at all. The responsibility Mama had mentioned grew suddenly heavier.

"Well, I'll teach you the one we used to say when I was a little girl and lived in this house," I said. "Repeat after me: 'Be present at our table, Lord. Be here and everywhere adored. These morsels bless and grant that we may feast in Paradise with Thee.' "

As I might have foreseen, even this simple grace brought forth a barrage of questions: Who was "Lord" and where was "Paradise"? I saw I had my work cut out for me.

For such young children, the little girls had exquisite table manners and were thoughtful and polite, treating me throughout our meal as if I were a special guest.

After we ate, I sat at the little white piano and played some simple songs, teaching them the words. They were so eager to please and I could see that, in spite of their lavish surroundings, they lacked many of the simple pleasures most children take for granted. My heart was bursting with tenderness for them, and right away, I was determined to give them everything I could to make up for whatever might be missing in their short lives.

The evening passed quickly and pleasantly. The children seemed eager to show me their pretty room and their dolls and toys and games, of which there were enough for ten children. They seemed hungry for companionship and relished the attention I gave them, babbling childishly about all the things that filled their days. I was pleased to see that Matty, their nurse, loved them with a fierce devotion. And when she had observed me with the children, she relaxed and took up her knitting as she rocked, obviously relieved that the three of us were getting on so well.

They clung to me as we said good night, as if they could not quite believe I would be there in the morning. As soon as I convinced them that they could peek in my bedroom door the first thing in the morning, they allowed Matty to lead them away to bed.

I walked down the hall to my own apartment, suddenly aware of a feeling of fatigue, an odd sense of depression. As I stood uncertainly in the middle of the room, I experienced that vague sensation of oppressive anxiety I had felt upon arriving at Montclair.

A tap on my door interrupted my melancholy reflection. It was Vinny, bringing hot water for a bath, and fresh towels.

"I hopes you rests well, Miss Dru," she said. "Sometimes it's hard to sleep peacefully the first night under a strange roof."

"But this isn't a strange roof, Vinny. You knew I lived here when I was a little girl, didn't you? I and Miss Alair — Mrs. Bondurant — and our cousin, Jonathan."

"Yes'm, I guess I do recollect hearin' about that," Vinny replied slowly. She stood quietly, alternately smoothing and pleating her white apron. "My grandmama was the cook here in the old days, and my mama and us lived here on the plantation during the War. I was jest a baby, but they tells me they hid the silver in the wagon when the Yankees come up here, unexpected, then set me on top!"

"Why, Vinny, I remember that!" I laughed. "Or I've heard Mama tell that story so many times that I *seem* to remember."

We smiled in mutual enjoyment of a long-ago joke we'd played on the "enemy."

Then Vinny's expression sobered. "They must have been happy times in the old days. Gramum often talks about it. I come here to work, first as a kitchen maid when I was ten, then later . . . Miss Alair choose me to be her maid." She shook her head, sighing. "I seen a lot of changes . . . lot of sadness."

Curiosity baffled with caution within

81

me. I was interested in what Vinny could tell me about Alair when she was mistress of Montclair . . . and about Randall. But I knew it was not wise to question servants or listen to backstairs gossip, nor should I encourage disloyalty in the servants of the man who was also my employer. Still, I had sensed that Vinny not only disliked her employer, but feared him. I wondered why. Despite my intense curiosity, caution won out.

"Vinny, I am tired," I admitted reluctantly. "After a nice bath, I should go straight to sleep."

Vinny turned to leave. At the door, she paused. "When my Gramum heard you was coming, she told me she'd be mighty pleased to see you again. She's got rheumatiz real bad, so she don't get around too good. You'd have to walk down to her cabin . . . that is, if you had a mind to —"

"I'd be happy to see her. Tell her I will come soon. I'm so pleased she remembered me."

Vinny still hesitated, apparently as eager to talk as I was to listen. But I felt strongly checked.

"Good night, Vinny," I said firmly.

"Good night, Miss Dru," she said, and

whisked out the door.

After I bathed, I blew out the lamp. Seeing that the newly risen moon had made the room almost as light as day, I went over to the window and looked out.

Planting my elbows on the windowsill, I leaned out, looking across the wide expanse of front lawn. The silvery line beyond was the river, with clumps of shrubs and small trees darkly etched against the deep blue of the evening sky.

I wondered how many times Alair must have viewed this same scene, with the sliver of a lemon-colored moon just beginning to show itself above the tops of the trees. Had she and Randall stood at the windows of the master bedroom and, arms locked around each other, gazed out? They must have been happy here together, I thought, sighing. Maybe they even walked hand-in-hand down to the river on summer nights. . . . Abruptly, I stopped my wild imaginings. What fantasy! I had seldom even seen Alair after her marriage. How could I guess what she had thought and felt?

I got up, closed the window, and went over to the bed. It had been turned down, the lacy coverlet folded on the needlepoint bench at the foot, the downy satin quilt folded in a triangle for ease in pulling up if the night grew chill. I was unaccustomed to such luxury.

My thoughts strayed again to Alair. She had grown up in the same poverty as I, and yet she had apparently made the transition to an opulent lifestyle with little trouble. Had become, in fact, extravagant! In all fairness, I supposed it would be quite easy to indulge oneself when everything was at one's fingertips.

I gave a little sigh, then turned over and snuggled into the down pillow, feeling myself drifting at last into a languorous sleep.

Sometime in the night, I awakened to a house that was silent, utterly still. A shaft of moonlight, spilling through the window, had fallen across my bed. It was this that had roused me, no doubt.

I shook off a nameless shiver of apprehension and drew up the quilt. How foolish to be frightened! At least six other people, besides two sleeping children, shared this roof.

Still, I could not help remembering Alair's untimely death. She was so young, I thought, much too young to die!

Resolutely, I closed my eyes, willing myself back to sleep. When I gave myself up to it, it brought curious dreams of a graceful figure in a wide crinoline skirt and pink parasol, circling endlessly to unheard music.

chapter
7

Two weeks after my arrival at Montclair, Randall called me into the library.

When I entered, he was standing at the long windows looking out on the sweeping vista of terraced lawns. He did not turn immediately, and I stood waiting for him to acknowledge my presence.

I was still very much in awe of Randall. His manner was so abrupt, so formal, so distant most of the time I could not imagine him as Alair's husband. How had he responded to her light-hearted teasing, her mercurial temperament, her playfulness? Perhaps it was because he missed these very qualities that he was generally melancholy.

At length he turned around and faced me. "So, then, are you settling in?" he demanded in an incongruously imperious tone. "Is everything to your satisfaction? Are you getting along with the children? Is there anything you need or want?"

The questions hurled at me, rapid-fire, quite startled me.

"Oh, no, sir! I mean, yes! Everything is fine, that is. The children are a joy, and we are getting along very well. As for my needs, I could not wish for anything more!" To my consternation, a furious blush mounted in my cheeks as I prattled on.

He pierced me with his penetrating gaze until I felt like an insect pinned under a microscope. "You're quite sure? You have only to say."

"Quite sure."

"Very well, then. You should know that I will be away on business." *A business trip? No one had mentioned that he would be leaving so soon after my arrival.* "You are to be in charge here during my absence, and the servants will answer to you. I've made that clear . . . although Benjamin pretty much runs the house and Cora, the kitchen, so you shouldn't be burdened."

Benjamin, I had learned, was the dignified butler who had been in Randall's service since long before he acquired Montclair or married Alair.

"Matty, of course, tends to the children's physical needs and Vinny —" Randall's mouth tightened slightly — "seems to manage everything else."

"Oh, you mustn't worry about a thing, sir," I said, attempting to reassure him. "How — how long do you plan to be away?" I could not resist asking.

Randall frowned. "I'm not sure. I have been invited to visit the Elliotts who are staying at the Springs, but I have not yet decided how long my stay will be."

The Elliotts! At once a picture came to mind — not a particularly pleasant one at that.

Before I left Thornycroft and while the Bondurants were still living in Massachusetts, Randall had suggested that I visit the children often, so as to get to know them better before I took over their full care at their home in Virginia.

On one such Thursday I was returning with them from an outing in the nearby park. Nearing the hotel entrance, I saw Randall with two ladies, awaiting the arrival of their carriage.

At our approach, the little girls rushed forward to greet their father, the two ladies making a great pretense of fussing over them. I might as well have been part of the scenery, for I received only the barest glance until Randall introduced me.

"This is the children's new governess,

Miss Druscilla Montrose," he said. "Mrs. Chalmers Elliott, Miss Peggy Elliott."

The introduction was received with a nod from the mother and a sidelong assessment from her daughter.

Peggy Elliott was indeed lovely — tall, with the hour-glass figure so admired at the time and displayed to great advantage by her stylish costume, a tightly fitted jacket of myrtle green wool trimmed with curly, black lambskin, the narrowed skirt pulled back into tiered pleats. She wore a little hat of matching fur tilted forward over her flaxen curls.

Her mother, an imposing woman but with none of her daughter's beauty, was elegantly attired in royal blue, with a sealskin cape and velvet bonnet.

I felt quite drab in my dove-gray pelisse and sensible bonnet alongside this fashionable duo. Unconsciously, I drew myself up and lifted my chin, regarding the pair with a steady gaze. It was a ploy I had adopted when some of my Yankee classmates tried to lord it over me. Outraged by their condescending manner, I had only to remind myself that I was a Montrose, one of the first families of Virginia.

But if her rude appraisal were not enough, on my way inside with the children, I had overheard Mrs. Elliott say to Randall, "Isn't she a trifle young? Are you sure you didn't make a mistake in dismissing Miss Ogilvie?"

Seething inside, I uttered a silent prayer for composure, and hurried past my employer and his guests. It was certainly no business of mine who Randall Bondurant chose as his friends, that is — and the thought struck me with icy horror — unless there were any possibility of Peggy Elliott ever becoming his wife and the children's stepmother!

Still, it was with a great deal of relief that I saw Randall make his departure. It was amazing how the atmosphere of the entire household lightened. Randall's restless personality affected all of us. I could understand how the tragedy of Alair's death still tormented him, but some of the tension I felt here seemed to dissipate with his leaving.

My new life as my little cousins' governess proved to be richly fulfilling. Actually, I was more a companion than governess because it had been decided to put aside any thought of lessons until fall. I woke up every morning eager to start my day with my small charges.

Both children were uniquely endowed

with special qualities that endeared them to me. Nora was obedient, creative, and charming; Lally, a mischievous imp, with a strong streak of independence combined with a sweetness that made her irresistible. As for me, I suppose I was so different from their former dour Scots governess that I was a pleasant change.

One thing disturbed me. The children had so many playthings that they had never found it necessary to resort to imagination. On the contrary, their mother and I, along with Jonathan, had possessed few toys, but spent marvelous hours pretending we were knights and fair ladies, or castaways on some desert island.

When I introduced such ideas to Nora and Lally, they were met with delight and I recognized the prospect of two active imaginations that matched my own.

I took the girls outside on sunny summer afternoons, and we picnicked in the woods or down by the wide creek that ran through the meadow. I even allowed them to take off their shoes and stockings and wade in the shallow water and, if the truth were known, did so myself on several occasions.

I was so busy and each day was so full that I had been at Bon Chance nearly a month before I found time to visit my father's grave in the Montrose family cemetery.

Late one afternoon while Matty was washing the girls' hair, I decided to slip away. I asked Tom, the gardener, if I could have some flowers, and he gladly cut me a lovely bouquet of yellow roses, being careful to get rid of all the thorns before handing it to me. He beamed with pleasure as I complimented him on the product of his diligent labor.

Carrying the bouquet, I made my way up the winding path to the top of the hill. From that vantage point, I had a breathtaking view of the valley — the rolling meadows, the ribbon of river shining in the sunlight, and in the far distance, a rim of blue mountains. It was so quiet I could hear only the hum of insects in the wildflowers, the slightest flutter of bird wings.

I opened the iron gate and stepped inside. Picking my way through the graves, I stopped here and there to read a headstone. All the people whose bodies lay here had lived, loved, and walked this very hillside to bury their own. All of them were bone of my bone, flesh of my flesh — my family.

And then I found the marker I was

looking for — a simple slab of granite stone with the chiseled words:

R.I.P.
Leighton Clayborn Montrose
1842–1865
Lieutenant CSA

"Faithful in love, Dauntless in War,
Where Shall We Find His Like Again?"
Sir Walter Scott

Reading the epitaph, I felt tears on my cheeks. My father was only a few years older than I was now when he died. I had heard my mother say over and over that she had had a year of perfect happiness, and who could say that of a lifetime? Imagine a love that even death could not diminish!

I laid the fragrant, dewy bouquet at the base of the headstone, whispering the age-old prayer: "Eternal rest give unto him and let perpetual light shine upon him."

I moved away and passed along the little graveled walkways searching for — I didn't know what until I realized it wasn't here. I stood absolutely still, knowing instinctively that I was in the spot where Alair's body had been laid to rest. But there was no gravestone! Dead over a year, and still no headstone erected to her memory?

How strange! Did Aunt Harmony and Uncle Clifford know there was no marker for their only, beloved daughter? Or had Randall, in his grief, forgotten that one must be commissioned, designed, ordered? I could not imagine the reason Alair's grave should go so long unmarked.

I was in a somber mood, indeed, when I walked down the hill back to the house, a mood that persisted past dinnertime and into the evening hours. I was peculiarly depressed as I went to bed that night and it took me a long time to go to sleep. My dreams were confused and though I slept heavily my sleep was not peaceful.

Suddenly an unearthly scream pierced the night and I awoke in mindless terror. The ear-splitting cry came again and, as I clutched the sheets to my chin, shuddering I remembered. Bondurant had imported peacocks. They stalked the grounds — regal, arrogant, unfurling their brilliant multicolored fan of feathers. I had forgotten. There was one old peacock still at Cameron Hall when I had come there as a child, the only one who had survived the more extravagant days. Now, I recalled the startling sound of their call.

But having been awakened so abruptly, I knew there was no immediate chance of my falling back to sleep easily.

The house was absolutely silent. There seemed no sound at all except that of my own shallow breathing. Through the windows came the pearly light from a late-rising moon shedding a milky opaqueness in the room, cloaking the furniture in unfamiliar shapes. I shivered, then realized my nightgown was damp with perspiration. I got up to change into a fresh one and, as I did, I heard something.

I stood quite still, straining to listen. From somewhere deep in the house came the sound of music.

I froze. Music? Who would be playing an instrument at this time of the night? And where was it coming from?

The fingers with which I was buttoning on my clean nightie were shaking. And I could still hear the unearthly notes in the distance. The melody seemed familiar. A waltz?

I was taught early that the only way to conquer fear is to face it. So I grabbed up my challis robe, flung it around my shoulders and, before I could change my mind, I opened my bedroom door and stepped out into the shadowy hall. I stood there listening for a minute, then still hearing the faint chords, I set out in the direction from which they seemed to be coming.

The hall floor beneath my feet was carpeted, so I made my way undetected to the children's rooms. Pausing at their door, I heard no one stirring and moved on cautiously.

At the end of a corridor in the adjoining wing, I saw a crack of light shining under a closed door.

It was a part of the house I had never seen. Somehow I had assumed this area was Randall's domain, so had steered clear. Now I was not so sure. I had seen Benjamin carrying out a breakfast tray the morning Randall had left. Later, I had noticed one of the maids carrying an armload of linens into that same room. Perhaps Randall slept downstairs.

As I crept quietly toward the closed door, the sound of the music became louder. Outside the door, I halted. My heart was pounding so loudly I could hear it. Then I put out my hand, felt the carved metallic doorknob, hesitated a second, then slowly turned it.

There was only a glimmer of light showing along the edge of the curtains as I stepped into the darkness. Underneath my bare feet I felt the lush softness of a velvety rug. A heavy scent like crushed roses hung in the air.

I crept across the room and groped for a pull to draw open the draperies. As I did so, the moonlight flooded in and the room leaped into view — the most beautiful room I had ever seen.

The bed was on a rounded dais, curtained in filmy lace, draped in satin, and mounded in ruffled pillows. An ornate mirror hung suspended over a skirted dressing table. On top was an array of perfume bottles, a set of silver and crystal toilette articles, a hand mirror, brush and comb etched with Alair's initials, ACB.

Moving quietly, I went over to the dressing table and lightly touched the glass top. It was then I saw the crêpe-de-chine peignoir flung over the back of the chaise lounge as if Alair had just tossed it there before dressing to go out. Involuntarily I shuddered. That movement was reflected in the mirror and I looked up and saw my image — wide-eyed, hair streaming about my shoulders, a haunted expression on my face.

I should get out of here, I thought, and turned to leave.

At the same time I realized the music had stopped.

My hands were clammy, my mouth dry. I can't remember ever being so terrified.

Then I heard the click of a door being closed. I pressed my hand to my mouth to stifle a scream. Even as an icy shiver rippled down my spine, I knew there must be some rational explanation. It was then I saw a piece of cloth caught in the door of the armoire.

Someone was hiding there! I reached for the silver hairbrush on top of the dressing table. Wielding it like a weapon, I crept cautiously toward the door, then yanked it open.

"Oh, Miss Dru!" a voice wailed and Vinny, huddling there, nearly tumbled out at my feet.

"Vinny! What on earth are you doing in here? Come out this minute!" Fear lent me a bravado I did not feel.

She crawled out and, burying her face in her hands, began to moan. Her voice was so muffled I could not understand a word she was saying. Soon I realized she was begging me not to punish her.

"No one is going to punish you, Vinny," I told her gently. "Just tell me what's going on."

Between sobs, gulps and sighs, the story unfolded. It seemed that after Alair's death, Randall ordered her room closed up, but Vinny was to come in and dust and air it weekly. She was not, however, to touch anything. He wanted everything to stay just as it was, nothing moved or changed.

As Alair's personal maid, Vinny had faithfully discharged this duty.

"I loved Miss Alair, Miss Dru. Some didn't understan' her, but I loved her anyway. And sometimes I come here . . . 'specially when Mr. Bondurant goes off . . . jest to be where she used to be, to look at her pretty things, her dresses and all. And sometimes I play her music box." She wilted beneath my stern gaze. "I knows it's wrong," she sobbed. "But somehow it make it seem lak she ain't daid. That she could come walkin' through the do' and tell me to lay out one of her party dresses!"

I patted her shaking shoulders. "All right, Vinny, don't cry anymore. I won't tell Mr. Bondurant, but you must promise not to come here in the middle of the night like this. To tell you the truth, you scared the wits out of me!"

Vinny got to her feet, wiping her eyes on her apron. "Yes'm, I is sorry. But sometimes Miss Alair, she seem so close. She loved the moonlight, she did. Sometimes she'd go out on the lawn and dance —"

"All right, Vinny," I said soothingly. "That's enough. You go on to bed now. We'll just leave and lock the door behind us. I don't think you should come in here any more except to do as Mr. Bondurant instructed you. Nothing more!"

"Yes, ma'am. The do' is kep' locked. I'se the only one who's got a key." She lifted her chin proudly. "Not eben Benjamin has one. Just me and Mr. Bondurant."

After I'd walked with Vinny to the door leading up to the servants quarters on the third floor, I went back to my own bedroom. But sleep was impossible.

I kept thinking of the locked room and the key in Randall's possession. Did he visit the room as Vinny had? Or did he keep it locked up tight, as effectively as his feelings? Apparently, he was still trying to escape the reality of Alair's death.

There were so many things I didn't understand — the unmarked grave, the shrine-like room, the concealed portrait. The more I learned about him, the more of an enigma Randall Bondurant presented.

Was he a man of no emotion or a man tortured by the past? Perhaps I would never know.

chapter
8

As abruptly as he had left, Randall returned, turning the whole household upside down.

He strode in, shouting for Benjamin and sending the maids scurrying in all directions. He sent for me to bring the children.

"I'm expecting guests," he announced summarily. "The Elliotts. I'm sure you remember Mrs. Elliott and her daughter from Boston? They are vacationing at White Sulphur Springs, and I've invited them here with their party of friends."

To say that I was overjoyed at this news would certainly be an exaggeration. My opinion of the Elliotts formed at our first meeting had not changed, nor did I think further association with these two ladies would alter it.

I tried to tell myself that their presence at Bon Chance for a day should make no difference to me. All I would be required to do would be to see that the children were properly dressed and brought down to be shown off to the company at tea time. Otherwise, I would stay demurely in the background as befit my position as governess.

I had not counted on Bondurant's unpredictable nature. What happened during the Elliotts' visit came as much of a surprise to me as to them.

From the vantage point of the upstairs balcony, the children and I watched the arrival of the Elliotts and their entourage. Accompanied by a middle-aged couple and their elderly relative, they alighted from their carriage in a flurry of boa feathers and ruffled parasols. We could hear their voices rising shrilly. I winced when I heard Mrs. Elliott's nasal twang.

"I must say, Mr. Bondurant, I do believe this to be the most authentic antebellum mansion I have yet seen."

Mrs. Elliott epitomized to me a familiar type I had seen parade into Cameron Hall Academy on Parents' Day. The mothers of some of my classmates, swathed in furs and aglitter with diamonds, would sweep into the "refined Southern atmosphere" in which they had enrolled their daughters and, within minutes, shatter their painstakingly achieved image.

Their arrogant manner, far from instilling awe, only revealed a crass self-centeredness. For that reason, people like Mrs. Elliott failed to impress me.

But in spite of the fact I'd told myself I cared not a fig what the Elliotts thought of *me*, I dressed very carefully that afternoon. I chose one of the new dresses Mama had made for me. Of fine muslin, it was trimmed with eyelet threaded with cornflower blue velvet ribbons.

My hair, ever a problem because of its lack of natural curl, was drawn back from my face and swirled into a simple figure-eight. But, to add a touch of elegance, I slipped in the small sapphire and pearl earrings Auntie Kate had given me when I left Cameron Hall. Satisfied with the effect, I went to get the children.

They looked adorable. Matty had brushed and curled their long golden hair and tied it with ribbons that matched their lilac satin sashes on the French embroidered lawn dresses.

Before long, Vinny appeared with the message that Mr. Bondurant was ready to present his daughters to his guests. Each of us took a small hand and proceeded down the circular staircase.

We could hear the voices of the company floating in from the veranda where they were seated to catch the breeze from the river on this warm summer afternoon.

Randall saw us at once, rose, and came forward to escort his two lovely little daughters out onto the shaded porch. I stepped aside, with dignity I hoped, and looked at a point above both of their heads as I felt the two Elliotts making a slow inventory of me.

I was holding myself so straight I felt my backbone stiffen. Indignation stirred within, but I maintained a serene smile. In a few minutes I could take the girls and leave, I told myself.

But I was wrong. To my astonishment, Randall drew up another chair for me. "I'm sure you remember my children's cousin, Miss Dru Montrose," he said in a bland tone.

Then he motioned me to sit down. Not wanting to create a scene by refusing, I hesitated a second then took a seat, fully aware of Mrs. Elliott's shocked expression.

I saw her exchange a glance with Peggy. The unspoken question passing between them was obvious to me, if to no one else. Giving me a perfunctory nod, both of them turned their entire attention to Randall and the little girls.

Randall had taken his seat, and Lally was

crawling up into his lap while Nora, leaning against his knee, was helping herself to the bon-bons on the low table beside him.

Suppressing my own discomfort, I began conversing with the elderly woman to my right who seemed grateful for the attention. I wondered if she had been ignored until now. Since she was slightly deaf, I assumed she had been left out of the others' conversation, intentionally or unintentionally. With me as her captive audience, she began a long recital of her rheumatic ills for which she was taking the waters at White Sulphur Springs.

As I listened with one ear to Miss Plimpton, I watched Peggy, who was in my direct line of vision. She was the complete coquette, I decided. It reminded me of some of the girls at school I had seen practicing in front of their mirrors. Flirting was a skill I had never acquired. But Peggy had perfected the art. She tilted her head, her eyes sparkled, and the dimples flashed on either side of her rosy mouth as she chatted with animation, fluttering her graceful white hands.

I did not venture a look at Randall to see how he was reacting to this display of charm. I gathered, however that he was enjoying it immensely.

At length, something was said about the lateness of the hour, and the ladies rose to leave. There was a general bustling about to collect handbags, shawls, and parasols and, as the company started through the hall back to the front where the carriage was waiting, I heard Mrs. Elliott chide Randall playfully.

"Now, dear boy, you must not be such a recluse here in this lovely retreat! You must come to see us at the Springs. There are dances every evening, pantomimes and magic lantern shows and tableaux! Such pleasant company, such delightful events. Now, promise we can look forward to your joining us there again soon."

I did not hear Randall's reply for just then Lally tugged on my hand, begging for another of the fancy iced cakes.

While Randall escorted his guests to their carriage, I took the children back upstairs. The afternoon had been a strain. I resented the awkward position I had been placed in, and was determined to avoid a recurrence of such a situation in the future.

The rest of the summer passed smoothly enough. Randall came and went. His trips lasted from a few days to two weeks, but I never knew if he took Mrs. Elliott up on her invitation.

Regardless of his whereabouts, I made sure that the children's routine was disturbed as little as possible. They needed at least one firm anchor in their little lives, I felt, and vowed to provide that security for them . . . even if their father wouldn't!

Nora was nearly nine and I knew, come September, I must outline a program of study for her. Lally, though only six, could read simple sentences already, and copied her older sister in every way. She, too, must begin lessons in the fall, I thought.

But in the last lovely days of summer, we made the most of our long afternoons. I used some of the time to tell Bible stories and teach the girls the beloved hymns and spirituals of my own childhood. Since that first evening, when I had learned to my dismay they had had little if any religious training, I had been careful to use every opportunity to introduce them to their heavenly Father and His loving care.

In our morning prayers, I encouraged them to thank the Lord for their blessings. Lally was quick to mention the tangible things — their toys, their books, their food — but Nora surprised me with an insight far beyond her years: "You must love us a lot, kind Father, to send us Dru!"

Recognizing the child's spiritual sensitivity, I pointed out the marvels of creation on our walks — birds, wildflowers, small woodland creatures, the very air we breathed — these and so many other delights that come from the hand of a caring Creator. They absorbed the truth like thirsty little sponges.

One thing puzzled me, however. Neither of the little girls ever spoke of their mother. I hesitated questioning them about her, for fear of causing them pain. It occurred to me that they had not seen very much of Alair in their short lives. Apparently, she and Bondurant had traveled a great deal and, while the girls were still very young, they had been left at home in Matty's devoted care.

What harm could it do, then, to teach them about their mother, I thought. So she was often in the stories I told them about our carefree days as children growing up at Montclair.

One day in early September, we were out in the garden where I had been instructing the children in the proper mixing of potpourri. Tom, the gardener, had allowed us to gather the fallen petals from the rose bushes he had pruned. After drying them in the sun, I helped the girls identify and gather herbs to be crushed and combined with the powdered rose leaves.

The herb garden had been planted by Noramary Montrose, the very first bride to make her home at Montclair. Born in England, she dearly loved gardening and took a special interest in herbs. In those early days, herbs were useful in many ways on the isolated plantation — in cooking, for medicinal purposes, as well as for their pungent aroma.

We were seated in the gazebo at the end of the garden path, pounding the ingredients with wooden spoons — rose leaves, lavender flowers, coriander seeds, orris root, cloves and cinnamon bark — then scraping them into the small linen bags we had made earlier and tying them with narrow ribbon.

Lally worked steadily, her chubby hands gathering the small piles of dried flowers and seeds and stuffing them into her bags. I watched her, the tip of her little tongue to one side of her mouth as she carefully filled the sachet bag, then pulled the ribbon tight. Her task completed, she held the bag up to her nose and breathed deeply. She closed her eyes, inhaling the spicy-sweet fragrance, then opened them wide.

"This smells like Mama!" she exclaimed.

Encouraged that this simple pastime had brought about spontaneous memories of Alair, I began gently to lead them to talk about their mother.

"She always smelled sweet," Nora added shyly.

"She was pretty too!" exclaimed Lally, warming to her subject. "And she danced! Sometimes she'd swing me around and around!"

Little by little, the children's remembered images brought Alair back. I wondered what they had been told about her death, but decided not to delve into what remained a mystery to all of us. Instead, I told them about heaven and how one day, we would all be together there.

That bright prospect pleased them, and thereafter, when Alair's name came up, it was naturally and with no embarrassment or discomfort.

Late one afternoon, as we were coming back from one of our impromptu picnics swinging our empty wicker baskets, we began chasing each other in a spontaneous game of tag. Running around the side of the house, we stopped short, laughing and breathless, at the sight of Randall standing at the top of the veranda steps. I had no idea how long he had been watching us.

I halted, attempting to tidy my hair that had fallen around my shoulders. What must Randall Bondurant think of his governess? The little girls, of course, had no such qualms. At the sight of their father, they dropped their baskets and greeted him happily.

"Papa! Papa! You're home!"

As usual, Bondurant had returned with no warning. I couldn't imagine why I found the idea so unsettling.

I left the children alone with him and went upstairs to put myself to rights. Since their father had been away so long, they were allowed to stay up long past the usual time for their bath and bedtime. But when it was nearly dark, the days still long in this Indian Summer, I went down to suggest that perhaps it was time for them to have some supper and get ready for bed.

I was always amazed at how Bondurant's usual stern expression softened whenever he spoke to his daughters and how affectionately they put their arms around his neck and kissed him good night. Their relationship was something rare and quite beautiful to see. It did, however, beg still unanswered questions about their mother.

The children were overstimulated by Randall's return, and it took Matty and me longer than usual to get them through their nightly routine. I stayed with them to hear their prayers and sat beside them, singing to them all their favorite hymns until at last they fell asleep.

When I eased out of their bedroom into the hall and quietly closed the door, I was startled to see Randall in the shadows, leaning against the balustrade.

"Oh, sir!" I gasped.

"Sorry, I didn't mean to frighten you," he said, stepping forward. His features, mellow by the light of the lamp kept burning on the hall table, were sharply defined, and I could not help thinking again how handsome he was. If I had not known better, I might have even suspected that the brilliance of his dark eyes was from tears.

His voice was husky when he spoke.

"I came up to say good night again, I didn't mean to eavesdrop, but I couldn't help overhearing them repeating the prayers you were teaching them. I stayed to listen . . . and to the singing —" He paused, and I held my breath. "You have a very pleasant voice, Miss Montrose."

"Thank you," I murmured, grateful that the dim light hid my blush.

"About the prayers —" He cleared his throat, and I felt a tautening in my stomach. Perhaps Randall was an agnostic. Perhaps he did not approve of my teaching the children to pray. Perhaps that was the explanation for their spiritual ignorance when I came here. I felt my hands grow clammy, and clenched them together tightly.

"My mother taught me those same prayers . . . when I was a child —" His voice thickened. "I'm afraid I was quite a disappointment to her."

He paused, then said, "But we cannot relive the past, undo our mistakes, can we? A rhetorical question I suppose you are too young to answer, Miss Montrose." He gave a short, derisive laugh. "Furthermore, I've been remiss in my daughters' religious training, but I see you are taking up the slack."

He turned as if to leave, then hesitated before adding, "I *am* grateful, Miss Montrose. You have brought something very . . . special to this house."

I stood there long after Randall's figure had disappeared down the stairway. My heart was pounding, his words echoing and re-echoing in my ears. For a brief instant, I had seen a side of Randall Bondurant that I had not even guessed existed.

Entirely unsummoned, the thought came into mind as if I had heard it spoken: *This is a man I could love.*

Even as it flashed into my mind, I rejected it. It was completely irrational. Randall was still mourning his wife. Our personalities, our positions in life were worlds apart. He was my employer; I, the governess to his children.

I walked back to my rooms, strangely moved by what had just transpired. Intuitively, I knew my relationship with Randall Bondurant had undergone a subtle change — the potential of which was dangerous.

I felt weak and vulnerable. Falling under the spell of this enigmatic man would be opening myself up to pain and disappointment. It would be risking heartbreak.

Mama was right! I should never have taken this position!

chapter
9

After that moment of rare intimacy between us in the shadowy hallway, Randall and I returned to our former, rather formal, relationship.

I made it a point never to be too often alone with him, nor to seek trivial excuses to consult with him. He continued to stop by the schoolroom in the mornings before he left for the day to inquire about the girls' progress with their lessons and, when he was at home, spent an hour or so in the later afternoon with them before supper and bedtime. Bondurant himself either dined alone or more often went out for the evening. Frequently, when I found it difficult to sleep, I heard his carriage wheels crunching on the shell drive below my windows late at night. Where and with whom he spent his long evenings I could only guess.

My routine with the children took on a pleasant pattern — lessons in the mornings, lunch, and afternoons spent in all sorts of varied pursuits. I combined outings with botany or French, trying always to make a game of whatever I was teaching. Both girls were quick and learned as fast as I could teach. It was an enjoyable, if uneventful, way to pass the days.

One such afternoon, we had started back to the house, when Nora gave me an impulsive hug. "Oh, Drucie, we never had such fun until you came!"

Lally quickly followed suit. "We love you, Drucie!"

"And I love *you!*"

Laughing and talking, we entered the house, only to be halted by the sound of loud, angry voices coming from the open library door. One was unmistakably Randall's. A violent quarrel seemed to be taking place.

Before I could think fast enough to remove the girls from the scene, we heard Randall's angry demand: "How dare you come here making such accusations?"

"I came because I have good reason to hold you responsible for Alair's death!"

"Get out of here! Get out of my house!" Randall ordered.

The children clutched my skirt, and I put trembling hands on their shoulders, drawing them close. We froze, not daring to pass the open door to reach the safety of the stairs. I thought of running back outside, but I could not move.

"*Your* house!" came the mocking taunt. "You mean the Montrose house you swindled away from the rightful owners, don't you? Why else do you think Alair agreed to marry you? To get back the property that belonged to her family, that's why! She didn't love you. She never loved you. It was *me* she loved!"

"Why you blackguard —" Randall shouted.

Then came the sound of scuffling, cries, grunts, the crash of breaking china, an overturned chair.

Frightened, I backed up against the wall, pulling the girls with me. They buried their heads in my skirt, and I could feel them shivering. *Dear God,* I prayed, *help us all.*

Suddenly we heard the thud of a body hitting the door, and I saw a man's back as Randall lunged toward him and gripped his shoulders.

The look on Bondurant's face was terrible to see. His eyes were wild, his expression savage. He grabbed the stranger and threw him against the door again, the crack of his head sounding like the sharp report of a gun.

Stunned by the blow, the man slumped forward, and Randall grasped him by the coat lapels and thrust him out into the hall.

"Now, get out of here! And if you ever set foot on this property again, I swear I'll kill you!"

The man stumbled and put out his hand to steady himself as he took a few staggering steps. He rubbed the back of his head and, when he brought his hand away, there was blood on his fingertips.

I managed to suppress the scream that rose in my throat. Too frightened to stir, all I could do was melt against the wall, clasping the children to me.

It was then the man turned and, for one horrible moment, we stared at each other. His face was flushed, contorted with anger and pain, but there was something disturbingly familiar about him. His eyes moved from me to the little girls, who were peering at him from the safety of my skirt.

He opened his mouth as if to speak, but at that instant Randall came to the library door, a towering figure of fury. "I told you to get out of here, Brett Tolliver!"

"I'm going," the other man snarled. "But

don't think you've heard the last of this! Don't think you can get away with murder!"

"*Out!*" Randall took two threatening steps forward.

Tolliver backed toward the front door, which stood open, shaking a raised fist at Randall. "Mark my words, Bondurant. You'll pay for what you've done. If it takes my last breath, I'll see that you do!"

I felt a deep shudder course through me. Still clinging to my legs through the layers of skirts and petticoats, the little girls began to cry. I could feel their small bodies shaking.

In the wake of Tolliver's departure, an odd stillness hovered. Except for the children's soft sobs, there was not a sound. We stood as immovable as statues until the sound of galloping horses' hooves faded away.

Then and only then did Randall become aware of us, huddled against the wall. A series of expressions crossed his face in quick succession — from the narrowed pinched look of hatred to a startled realization that we were witnesses to the dreadful scene, followed by consternation that the children had overheard everything.

He paled until his hawk-like features

seemed chiseled from granite. He ran one hand through his hair and shook his head as if to clear it.

Then he spoke to me sharply. "Take the children upstairs." With that directive, he turned on his heel, went back into the library, and slammed the door behind him.

The little girls stared up at me, bewildered.

"Why was Papa so angry?" Nora asked piteously.

"Who wath that bad man?" whispered Lally, her lisp more pronounced because of her fright.

"Hush, hush, my darlings," I soothed. "I'm sure it has nothing to do with us. Perhaps your Papa will explain later. I think we should just try to forget it." I must think of something to erase that awful scene from their impressionable minds. "Come, let's do what Papa said. Let's go upstairs and ask Vinny to bring us some nice tea. I think Cora made some poppyseed cake this morning. . . . I'll play the piano . . . we can sing."

I was talking as fast as the thoughts occurred to me, trusting I had enough influence with the children to make them believe everything was going to be all right, to help them forget the frightening adult anger to which they had been exposed.

But although it was easier to distract the children than I had expected; for myself, it was quite impossible.

Brett Tolliver! Of course he did not recognize me. It had been almost ten years since he had seen me. And then I had been only a child.

The last time I had laid eyes on him was at Alair's wedding. The garden had been in exquisite bloom. At one end, a bower had been erected as an improvised altar. The rest of the garden had been transformed for the reception, a striped tent over the bridal table, with floral garlands looped along the lace cloth and a tiered wedding cake in the center. A platform had been built, its floor sanded and polished for dancing, while a small orchestra played throughout the afternoon.

I remember sitting with the aunties, eating cake and lemon sorbet and watching the dancers. How perfectly lovely Alair was that day, whirling in her white gown and crinoline petticoats, her golden hair glistening in the spring sunshine. I had heard the whispers, seen the raised eyebrows as, one after the other, she had danced with all her old beaux.

Then Brett Tolliver had sauntered

through the gathering and, ignoring the next young man in line, had taken Alair in his arms for the waltz just beginning.

They looked wonderful together — the two blonds — both unbelievably beautiful as they circled, dipped, moved with absolute grace. They looked as if they had been born for this moment.

Randall had finally intervened at a pause in the music and exchanged some words with Alair. Afterward, however, Brett and Alair continued their dancing, and Randall moved to the edge of the pavillion and stood stoically watching them.

It was a story I had forgotten until now.

Of course, after the terrible scene, other memories came flooding back. I knew that Brett Tolliver and my cousin had been childhood sweethearts. Alair had confided in me once that they were "promised" to each other, that they had carved their names in hearts on the big elm tree in the meadow at Montclair.

But Tolliver was no longer the Greek god of that long-ago wedding day. His burnished blond hair had thinned, and the slim, athletic build had thickened. His once-handsome face was mottled with anger and his speech seemed crude and vulgar.

I realized the accusation had been spoken in anger, frustration, and probably in unhealed grief, but what had Brett meant when he had said, "I hold you responsible for Alair's death" and "You can't get away with murder"?

I shuddered, recalling the naked fury, the unbridled emotions I had observed in both men.

Somehow the evening ended. I was exhausted with the effort of pretending a gaiety I didn't feel. At last I got the children into bed, said prayers, and kissed them good night.

Just as I was leaving their room, Vinny came up the stairs. "Mr. Bondurant . . . he want to see you, Miss Dru. He in the library."

When I entered the library, Randall was sitting at his desk, his chin resting on his hand. He seemed deep in thought. With only one lamp burning, his classic profile was outlined against the green velvet draperies drawn on the window behind him.

"You wanted to see me, sir?"

He turned his head, frowning, as if trying to remember who I was. "Yes, Miss Montrose." When he spoke, it was crisply and decisively. "I've decided to close the house. I plan to go to Italy for the winter."

He rose and began to pace while I absorbed this new information. "I want you to get the children ready, their clothes packed, whatever they need. We'll go to New York first, then get the first sailing date we can. I don't fancy an Atlantic crossing any later than October. So, make the necessary preparations at once."

I was stunned by the suddenness of the decision. But I had learned not to question Randall Bondurant.

"I think the girls will benefit from a milder climate," he remarked as if in explanation as I was leaving the room.

A milder climate was hardly the reason for this abrupt move! Had Brett Tolliver's threats precipitated this decision? Or was Randall Bondurant escaping his own tortured past?

chapter
10

Early the next week, with Randall's permission, I prepared for a visit to Richmond to see Mama before leaving Virginia for the Continent. The children would be in good hands with Matty and Vinny, so I left on a Thursday, planning to return to Mayfield several days later. Randall had already made our train reservations to New York from where we would embark for Europe.

I wondered how Mama would receive the news that I would be spending an indefinite period of time in Italy.

"Oh, my darling girl!" she exclaimed when I told her, one delicate hand fluttering to her throat. "What an opportunity of a lifetime! I always longed to go to Italy myself. In fact, Lee — your father and I spoke of it many times. We dreamed of going there 'after the War.' But our dreams were destined not to come true. Now, our daughter will be able to live out the dream. I am so happy for you, dear, but —"

"But what, Mama?"

"— afraid for you, too. Perhaps I shouldn't say this, but it seems you are becoming more and more . . . involved with Bondurant and his children." She paused as if hesitant to go on.

"But that's only natural, isn't it, Mama? Besides the children need me so —"

"I understand that . . . but to live in a foreign land . . . He *has* rented a house there, you say?" At my nod, she added, "For how long?"

"That I don't know, Mama. Some American friends who winter there every year have found a villa on the outskirts of Rome."

"Rome!" again Mama exclaimed. "Imagine such a thing!"

Her excitement was evident in the sparkle of her eyes, the delicate flush of her cheek. But I had no idea why she still harbored some reservations.

"Randall —" At her lifted brow, I corrected myself, "*Mr. Bondurant* wants the girls to be exposed to all the arts — art and architecture, the language, the history —"

"It would seem then that he would hire an Italian governess, wouldn't it?" Mama asked mildly.

"But the girls are used to *me*, Mama.

They have become very fond of me. I think their father realizes that and believes as I do, that they must have some continuity in their lives."

Mama made no reply, but continued to look thoughtful.

Much of my visit was spent in looking over my wardrobe, deciding what would be suitable to take with me, what needed refurbishing or replacing. With my generous new salary, we were able to shop for fabrics, and Mama set about making me some new outfits.

During the days of cutting out, fitting and assembling my wardrobe, Mama and I spoke of many things. I did the basting of the garments, while she concentrated on the fine sewing and finishing.

One afternoon, toward the end of my time in Richmond, I casually brought up the name of Brett Tolliver. I purposely omitted any mention of the frightful scene I had witnessed in the hope of learning further details of his romance with Alair.

"It's very sad, really," Mama nodded, looking up once or twice from her sewing. "He and Alair seemed meant for each other. They were so alike — handsome, fun-loving, adventuresome, and yes, impetuous. But no one could help loving them both." She sighed and stopped to thread her needle.

"I don't know exactly what happened. When Clint failed at yet another business and Harmony's health began to deteriorate, I saw Alair change. As their only child, I think she felt the burden of making life a little easier for her parents." Mama lifted the pleated skirt she was stitching, turned it, and began working on the other side.

"I'm not sure just when and how she met Randall Bondurant. Alair was very popular, invited everywhere, to every home in Mayfield. But I think she met him at a social held at one of the old houses bought up by some of the . . . new people." Mama gave a little frown and pursed her lips, thinking no doubt of the Yankee invasion of the South after the War. Then she shrugged. "Anyway, the man pursued her persistently. The courtship was very short. I think Alair was dazzled by his wealth, his power to give her everything she had ever dreamed of, and to provide security for her parents as well."

"Don't you think she loved him then?" I asked cautiously.

"Love? Love has many faces, Dru. I think she was fascinated, infatuated, but in love . . . I don't know."

"But what about Brett?"

"Oh, he was devastated." Mama shook her head. "Everyone was afraid he might do something reckless. Such a headstrong boy! We all held our breath at the wedding, I can assure you."

"I remember." I nodded. "At least I think I was aware of the stir he created."

Mama bit off the end of a thread. "Afterwards, he went out west, you know. Became a cowboy for a while, we heard. I think he even went to California to try his hand at gold-mining. He came back here when his father died."

"What then?"

Mama gave a deep sigh. "Well, the Tollivers had lost everything — their land, the house. The new owners hired Brett on for the stables. He lives above them. A sad end for a proud man. Brett is one of the real casualties of the South's defeat. He grew up where there was nothing for a young man to hope for."

"But Mama, look at Uncle Rod. He was actually in the War. Yet he's made a successful life for himself."

"Rod is a survivor in the best sense of the word," she declared firmly. "But he's had his own defeats —"

I wanted to get back to the subject of Brett Tolliver and his relationship with Alair. "But if Alair really loved Brett, why didn't she marry him? Maybe she could have helped him make something of his life."

"Alair looked delicate, fragile even. But she was a stubborn little thing. I think she made up her mind to accept all that Randall Bondurant had to offer."

I let a full minute go by before asking another question. "So what does Brett Tolliver do now?"

My mother looked up, an ambivalent expression on her face. "You mean besides imbibe strong spirits?"

"He drinks?"

"Heavily, sad to say. Nominally, he is caretaker for the estate that used to belong to his family. The new owners travel a great deal. But, mostly, I understand he drinks, broods. . . . But, come now, surely there's a more pleasant topic of conversation. Do tell me about the little girls —"

So we left the subject of Brett Tolliver. But I had a clearer picture of him now, of what he had become, and why he had come to Bon Chance that day and confronted Randall so wildly. His allegations were probably the product of his own liquor-clouded mind, the fevered imaginings of a bitter, morose drunk. He had lost Alair long ago, but kept their young love alive in his tormented heart. If Randall knew all this, why had he reacted so strongly? Why had such idle threats prompted him to uproot us all and leave the country?

For the rest of the afternoon, I regaled Mama with accounts of the Bondurant sisters — their precocity, their unexpected wit and charm, their surprisingly mature prayers. But in the very midst of this recital, a part of my mind was occupied with the perplexing puzzle of the strange romantic triangle.

As the day of our actual parting dawned, I think Mama and I both realized how long it might be before we saw each other again.

"I wish *you* were coming," I told her, taking both her hands in mine. "I wish we were going to see Italy together. It isn't fair. You would so love to see the museums, the art galleries, the great cathedrals —" I raised her small hand to my cheek lovingly.

Tears brightened her eyes for a moment, but she smiled at me. "You must write letters, tell me everything you see, experience, feel. That way, I can travel with you."

"Oh, I will, Mama! I promise."

As she helped me pack, she said, "I think Garnet will be in England in the spring. She and Jeremy often go to the Continent as well. Perhaps there will be a chance for you to see her. I should think that by then you would welcome a familiar face from home."

Suddenly a thought occurred to me, and I suppose my indignation showed. "Why hasn't Aunt Garnet invited you to visit her? She could well afford it!" It seemed odd to me that these two sisters-in-law, who had shared responsibilities, sorrows, and frustrations during the War, now lived in such different worlds.

Mama looked shocked. "But she has, dear. Many times. It just isn't possible to leave Auntie Nell."

I looked at my mother, thinking of Aunt Garnet's life of ease and affluence compared to Mama's service to others, and pondered the curious disparity of their paths. Did my mother never envy nor wish she could trade places with Aunt Garnet?

I bit my lip. But Mama, quick to discern my thoughts, leaned over and patted my cheek. "Don't worry about me, darling. I am happy and content. Believe me. Read

Philippians 4:11 and you'll understand." She went on folding the beribboned cotton chemises. "I decided early on that I would not be overcome by circumstances, that regardless of events in my life, I would simply trust the Lord and try to be happy. Life is not easy for anybody, Dru. Appearances are often deceiving, and what may seem like perfection to outsiders often masks secret sorrows."

She then turned to the ruffled petticoats and started placing them in neat piles on top. "It's best to look upon life as a challenge. Then, whatever we are given, we can remember that others are looking to us for example, and that helps us to be strong and courageous."

I went over to her then with the tears streaming down my face. Holding her close, I murmured, "Mama dearest, how very wonderful you are."

"Nonsense!" Her voice took on a stern note, then she laughed that light, girlish laugh that had not changed with the years. "Now that's enough sermonizing for today. Let's wait until Sunday and see what wisdom Reverend Miller will impart."

On the train back to Mayfield Monday morning, I thought about the church service we had attended the day before and realized that what Mama had said to me had stamped itself more strongly on my consciousness than the minister's words.

The hymn selected had, however, affected me profoundly. Music always ministered to me and, along with the clickety-clack of the train's wheels on the steel rails, the lyrics rang in my mind.

Wide as the ocean, deep as desert sands,
God's love reaches, God's love extends.
Tho' we travel to far-off lands,
Cross uncharted seas,
His love follows unreservedly.
No matter the distance,
It can be anywhere,
God's love reaches,
We are always in His care.

I prayed that was true, that the "blessed assurance" I had been taught to believe in would sustain me in whatever lay ahead. For the first time since Randall had announced our destination, however, I felt a tiny tickle of fear.

Part II
September 1883

chapter
11

September 1883

Dearest Mama,

We took the children on deck for their first sight of land after nearly two weeks at sea. They have been good sailors throughout this long journey, but naturally we all long to set our feet on solid ground once more. Gibraltar!

One of the ship's officers, Lt. Mason, who has been very kind and attentive the whole trip, came alongside us while we stood at the railing to point out Spain on one side of the ship, Africa on the other. Imagine!

The harbor was full of ships, yachts, and little boats. We were to have a full day here while our ship took on fresh supplies, so Randall hired an open carriage with a fringed canvas top, and we rode through the town, which is much larger and more picturesque than I had imagined. I wished for my paintbox more than once, for I'd have loved to capture this place in water-colors.

Everywhere I looked was a perfect landscape — fascinating narrow, little streets; brilliant flowers; and, surrounding us, the beautiful blue of the Mediterranean, rimmed by the bold profile of the mountains.

All too soon we had to hurry back to make the six o'clock departure of the ship. I stood at the railing again as we steamed away between the coasts of two continents!

Ever your loving daughter,
Druscilla

September 1883

Dearest Mama,

The sky was cloudy and overcast when we sailed into the Bay of Naples, and I thought to myself, "Where is the sunny Italy I've heard so much about?"

Then we anchored and were soon surrounded by small boats, filled with Italian sailors in flamboyant attire, all chattering and shouting to us and to one another. Of course, we couldn't understand a word they were saying, but it was all very exhilarating. I felt as if we were actually at the end of our long journey.

We drove through the noisy, crowded streets to our hotel, which is really quite grand. The girls and I have a lovely suite of rooms. We lunched on the terrace, now in bright sunshine, and Randall suggested we take a drive to San Marino.

The town rests atop a long, winding hill from which we had a magnificent view of Naples. There is this marvelous blue haze with the sun glistening through clouds. At last, we saw the spectacle Randall had promised — Vesuvius itself! Every day brings new surprises! One day soon we shall go to Pompeii.

Ever your loving daughter,
Druscilla

October 1883

Dearest Mama,

We are now at the Villa Florabella, the house Randall has rented for our stay. I will try to describe it, though I shall not do it justice. It deserves to be experienced!

A long line of cypress trees leads from a scrolled iron gate up to the house, a large imposing structure of terra-cotta stucco, with tile roof and white marble accents. In the entrance hall, there are twisted columns of white marble veined in purple, and beautiful mosaic tile floors. All the rooms have high ceilings — even higher than the rooms at Montclair — and tall windows, looking out on terraces and gardens, which are themselves works of art — winding paths with pools and fountains, statues in curved niches in the walls, flowers and brightly blooming plants everywhere!

Inside, you have to wonder if this villa once belonged to a Roman senator or perhaps a prince. The furniture is very elaborate, and I feel sure the paintings are priceless. The walls and ceilings are painted with scenes, many of them the artist's ideas of celestial dwellings. Cherubs abound, along with garlanded mirrors, inlaid tables, and gold-leafed and tapestried chairs.

I cannot imagine ever thinking of this place as "home," but someone once did! There is an aura of antiquity about the place. What stories could be told by these silent stones.

At the end of the garden steps, a path winds up a gentle hill. From there we have a view of Rome!

I can hardly wait to begin seeing it. Randall means for us to explore the city, and we will plan many little trips after we are more settled. He is hiring a tutor to instruct us in Italian, which will be very helpful in dealing with the servants here as well as with merchants, carriage drivers, and other natives.

Rosalba, a lovely young girl with eyes like black olives, is to be personal maid to the girls and me. Nora and Lally already adore her and she is wonderful with them. She told me in her halting English that she had eight younger brothers and sisters and so is quite experienced in caring for children.

So, dear Mama, you can see that this is going to be not only an exciting adventure, but an educational experience. I intend to master the language in order to appreciate the culture, the arts, the music of Italy so much more . . . and to better share it with you!

Ever your loving daughter,
Druscilla

November 1883

Dearest Mama,

Our Italian lessons are going quite well. Signor Pietro Orsini is a charming young man with sad dark eyes, a courtly manner, and a delightful way with the children.

When we stumble and make mistakes when trying to converse in Italian, he is most gentle in his correction. We laugh a great deal, because many of the words sound alike. But when we mispronounce them, our version produces an entirely different meaning, which he points out to us.

I have been intrigued by Signor Orsini's background. He has such a noble bearing, such exquisite manners, and his accent is perfect, unlike the speech of the servants. I could not help wondering why a man of such obvious breeding should hire out as a tutor.

Today I learned something about the circumstances in which he now finds himself. It seems that, while he was a student at the university, Signor Orsini became involved with some Revolutionary groups, even worked on a paper put out by people seeking a more democratic form of government. Since his family is an old and prestigious one, his association with these groups enraged his father. Consequently, they are estranged, and he is cut off from any support from his family and so maintains himself by giving music lessons and tutoring.

He is so immensely intelligent, so intense, yet still works for change in the status quo that I quite admire him. But he has a struggle just to survive, I gathered, although he is in no way self-pitying nor resentful. He said he understands his father's feelings even if they cannot agree.

Somehow this put me in mind of our family's former attitude toward Randall Bondurant. At least, I hope this estrangement is in the past, for he has been very considerate of me —

Ever your loving daughter,
Druscilla

December 1883

Dearest Mama,

What a lovely day! We have just returned from a visit to Florence, where we drove through the hills above the town. The hillsides are dotted with silvery olive trees — groves and groves of them! All along the way, groups of peasants in colorful dress waved and smiled at us as we passed in our open carriage.

At the top of one hill overlooking the town, we enjoyed a basket picnic lunch. From there, the town looked like a toy village, with tiny pink and yellow stucco houses strung together with streets like silver ribbons. We were ravenous and dined on delicious crusty Italian bread, thin sliced ham, cheeses of many kinds, and luscious fruit. No wonder so many of the Italian women are amply built! I'm hoping not to outgrow the lovely frocks you made for me just before we sailed!

The view beyond the town itself was glorious — the valley of the Arno and Campagna stretching off like a rolling sea, crested with waves of blue hills and snow-capped mountains. I made a quick sketch which I shall later try to paint.

Ever your loving daughter,
Druscilla

January 1884

Dearest Mama,

Your letters came today and what a welcome sight was your handwriting on the envelopes! I can't believe I have been away so long, and that Christmas has come and gone in Virginia, while it is like summer here!

You ask what a typical day is like for me here. I'm ashamed to admit that the sun is already up and shining by the time I awaken. The children have usually had their breakfast and are playing out in the garden under Rosalba's watchful eye while

I am having breakfast on the little balcony outside my bedroom. I'm sure you think I am growing quite spoiled amid all this "Roman decadence"!

Seriously, after a leisurely beginning — so different from Thornycroft — my days are very full and scheduled.

Signor Orsini comes at ten for our Italian lessons and often accompanies us on some planned expedition. Since he knows Rome so well and of course is so fluent in the language, he is the ideal guide when we visit a museum or church or gallery. Since the girls' attention span is short, they seem tired or bored. I occasionally send them home with Rosalba, then I continue my guided tour with Signor Orsini.

I have been concerned that we might be taking up too much of his time on these excursions, for which he is not being paid by Bondurant, but he assures me that it is his pleasure to introduce others to the Italian treasures he loves so much.

Besides, he does not go to his job at the printing plant until late in the afternoon. I don't know when the poor man gets any sleep. Sometimes I think he looks so haggard, with shadows under those mournful dark eyes. He is also much too thin, and I have suggested to Rosalba to bring coffee and pastries up to us after our lesson in the mornings. I notice that Signor Orsini relishes these treats, and I'm glad if we can supplement what must be the meager diet he is able to afford on his small salary!

Christmas in Italy is in great contrast to our Virginia celebrations. I'm sure you would think the customs very strange indeed, though they seem appropriate for this setting.

In Italy, Christmas is not especially a time for exchanging gifts. People go to church, have family dinners, pay visits and send nosegays, violets being the flower of choice. To Italians, these speak the language of romance, and young men here send them to their *amoratas* or fiancées.

The celebration of Christmas begins weeks ahead of the date we mark. It is festival time for the peasants who come down from the hills to participate in a novena, or nine days of religious activity and gaiety. They have parades, carry banners and statues, play a sort of bagpipe, blow brass horns, and sing for hours on end.

Of course, I felt it important to keep some of our own traditions. So the girls hung their stockings on their bedposts on Christmas Eve, and Randall filled them with lovely presents he had ordered for them.

I took them to the small Anglican church for a service that seemed very quiet and formal compared to the noisy celebrations in the streets. Since the chapel is quite near our villa, we walked home and were surprised to find Signor Orsini waiting at the gate.

He had brought gifts for both girls and presented me with a little bouquet of violets, which both surprised and touched me. I realized at once that because of the rift in his family, he would probably be spending the holiday alone. So, impulsively, I asked him to join us for our lunch.

Being separated from my own dear family makes me especially sensitive and compassionate to his situation, I suppose. And his instant acceptance and obvious gratitude for the invitation made me feel, spontaneous though it was, that it was the right thing to do.

Randall was dining with friends and would be gone for the evening. He has met a group of Americans and Englishmen who winter in Italy, and has become socially involved with them. They ride together in the mornings, lunch at the various villas, and go sightseeing together.

The evenings are filled with all sorts of entertainment — dinner parties, soireés, concerts, balls and of course, the opera. Since Randall seems happier than I have ever known him, I must assume that this kind of life is the answer to his moodiness and melancholy so apparent the last month we were in Virginia.

To finish about our Christmas — After we had lunched on the terrace in the lovely sunshine — I imagine Richmond and Mayfield were blanketed in snow? — the little girls played with their new Christmas toys, setting up a tea table for their big, wax dolls with real curls Randall had ordered from France. Signor Orsini and I walked along the shady paths of the garden conversing — in Italian!

As I told you before, he is so interesting and knows so much about the history and art of his native country that I am learning a great deal I would not have learned in all the guidebooks and histories I could read about Italy.

At the day's end, he thanked me profusely for sharing our Christmas with him, kissed my hand in the Continental manner, and invited me to call him "Pietro," since Signor Orsini seemed too formal for friends.

I hesitate to do so, especially in front of the little girls who are, after all, his students. But perhaps, when we are in private conversation, it would be all right. What do you think, Mama?

Ever your loving daughter,
Druscilla

February 1884

Dearest Mama,

Randall announced we were to go to Pompeii this week, so I prepared the girls with the story of that fateful city so that they would understand better what we were about to see.

I thought I had prepared myself, too. But it was a fearful experience. Our guide pointed out that the ruts in the street were actually made by the chariot wheels of those who were attempting to escape from the lava flow. What must it have been like on that terrible day when the volcano erupted and poured streams of molten fire through the hills and over the town as people tried to flee? How awful to have one's life snuffed out in a single moment of horror!

I was quite subdued on the trip back. I could only think how suddenly life can end. It didn't matter if they were happy or unhappy that day. In a flash, everything was over for them!

Naturally, Alair came to mind and how one day she was vibrantly alive, out riding her beloved horse, and the next she was dead!

We must, I think, enjoy each day, each minute we're alive and above all be kind and loving to everyone. Life is too short for disagreements and estrangements!

Ever your loving daughter,
Druscilla

March 1884

Dearest Mama,

I know it has been a long time since my last letter. My only excuse is that each day seems to hold more than the last. We have taken several short trips that I can only briefly mention, since description of the beauties of these ancient cities seems inadequate at best.

Still, I would be remiss if I failed to tell you about Rome, the Eternal City! What a profound experience! Pietro — Signor Orsini — has been so gracious to escort me to some of its most famous landmarks, and his knowledge adds such a personal touch. The light in Rome is so different from anything I've ever seen that it is no wonder it inspired so many great works of art! The mellow gold from the dome of St. Peter's Cathedral touches all the buildings, the walls, the pillars with a dreamlike quality. Even the River Tiber seems made of liquid amber.

The Sistine Chapel was beyond my wildest dreams — the scope, the figures, the exquisite detail. And the fact that Michaelangelo painted most of it while lying on his back!

We went to Florence again. Some friends of Randall were going and so he wanted us along. This time I got away for an afternoon, since they had brought their governess for their children — a boy and a girl about the same age as Nora and Lally. I went to Uffizi, but it was so crowded with other tourists it was hard to appreciate the pictures.

Randall asked me to dine with them, but I refused, saying I preferred to be with the children. He seemed annoyed, but he doesn't realize that he places me in an awkward position with people who think a governess is little more than a servant. Even though he always introduces me as his children's cousin, I feel more comfortable to retain my independence — and my dignity.

Having said that, you will understand how I feel about the next piece of information. The Elliotts have come to Rome! You remember my telling you of that mother and daughter? Well, they have leased a villa quite near ours, and I assume there will be much visiting and entertaining back and forth.

I know you think I am being uncharitable, Mama, and perhaps I am. I should be more faithful in my daily devotional reading and remind myself frequently of how Paul admonishes us to treat our "enemies." (I'm not sure why I used that word in regard to the Elliotts!)

To turn to a much pleasanter topic, I must tell you of a rare and beautiful experience Pietro made possible. One day as he was leaving after our Italian lesson, he asked if I would like to see the Colosseum.

"Oh, yes, indeed!" I replied. "It is the one place all Christians count as the most important building in Rome — the place where Christian martyrs died for their faith."

At this, Pietro looked somewhat embarrassed. Then he corrected me very gently, "Actually, the martyrs did not perish in the

Colosseum. This was the arena where entertainment for the Caesars was held — the great spectacles, the circuses, the gladiator fights, chariot races —"

So much for pietistic pronouncements from the uninformed!

Well, Mama, needless to say, it was an unprecedented experience. The Colosseum is huge, having a seating capacity of over five thousand people at one time. It makes all you have read of the history of that period come alive.

I must stop for now. God bless and keep you, dearest. Give my love to Aunt Nell, and to the Camerons when you see them and Aunt Garnet, too, if she's visiting in Mayfield.

Ever your loving daughter,
Druscilla

chapter
12

What I didn't confide to Mama in my last letter to her were the true circumstances of my visit to the Colosseum. And of course I wouldn't dream of telling her what happened upon my arrival back at Villa Florabella!

Properly chastened by Pietro's greater knowledge of early Christian history, I was a little taken aback when I realized we would be visiting the ancient ruin together.

"There is a full moon this week, Signorina Dru," he told me happily. "It is one of the loveliest sights possibly in the world."

Perhaps it was rash to accept his invitation, perhaps even improper, but I was already committed. He would call for me at nine the following evening. I had many second thoughts, as well as some fluttery misgivings. On the other hand, it would hurt Pietro's feelings if I made some flimsy excuse now.

The children were sound asleep, with

Rosalba knitting in the next room, when I slipped out of the house and down to the gates to await Pietro's arrival. I worried that he had spent more money than he could afford to hire a carriage, but it was too late to fret about that.

Randall was out for the evening — to the Elliotts' I think — although I certainly did not question him about his plans when he came up to say good night to Nora and Lally, since I was unwilling to discuss my own.

To see the Colosseum by moonlight transcended anything I have yet experienced. Seen in the mysterious, silvery light, its vastness was almost overpowering. Looking down the pyramided rows into the cavernous depths, I was thrust back in space and time — imagining the roar of the crowds, the thunder of racing horses' hooves, the pulsing frenzy of the crowds!

We stayed there much longer than I realized. Pietro, always sensitive, had remained a little apart from me as I had sat on one of the stones high above the amphitheater, deeply moved by my experience. So many thoughts rushed through my head as I recalled what had taken place in this spot — all the lives of all the people who had come there as spectators, all the history these crumbling stones had witnessed. Whether or not the martyrdom of the saints had actually occurred within these walls, the beginnings of Christianity were vitally linked to this place.

We were both quiet as we rode back to the Villa. The moon had risen high by the time we reached the gates, the tall cypress trees casting elongated shadows upon the stucco walls surrounding the villa.

"Let me out here, Pietro," I said as he reined the horse. "And thank you so much — gratia —"

Pietro turned toward me, the moon illuminating the contours of his handsome face, obscuring the dark eyes. Before I knew what was happening, he took my hand and pressed it against his cheek, murmuring something in Italian. I could understand only one phrase: "Cara mia."

I drew in my breath as Pietro turned my hand over and kissed my palm. The feel of his lips sent a shiver all through me, and I drew it gently away.

"Have I offended?" he asked. "I meant only to convey how much I care for you — It gives me such happiness just to be with you."

"Oh, Pietro — Signor Orsini, you mustn't —"

"Forgive me. I could not help myself. If I have offended —"

"No, it's not that, it's —" I stumbled over my words, not knowing what to say. "I must go in now. It is very late." I was breathless, confused. This was something I had not expected, though perhaps I should not have been so hopelessly naive.

He got out, came around the other side and gently helped me down. "Mia — Dru —" he began, and I rushed to halt any further declarations.

"I must hurry now. Thank you again. We'll see you on Monday for lessons." With that, I pushed through the gate and hurried along the shadowy tree-lined road and into the garden.

Even though the night was warm, I was shivering. This had been a highly emotional evening — my almost spiritual experience at the Colosseum, then the unexpected scene with Pietro — How would this change things? I hoped it would not make our lesson times together uncomfortable. I had not allowed him to continue whatever he might have wanted to say, for I wasn't sure I was ready to hear more.

So intent was I upon my own turbulent emotions that I was halfway up the terrace steps on my way into the house when a tall figure blocked my way.

"Well, Miss Montrose, what brings you out in the moonlight? A late errand, or a rendezvous with a lover?"

Startled, I nearly stumbled and a strong hand grasped my elbow to steady me. It was Randall. I could not see his face in the shadows so I couldn't tell if he were angry or amused. His voice was tinged with the sarcasm I'd noticed so often — sometimes directed at himself, sometimes at others.

"Oh, sir!" I gasped. "Neither! I mean, I have just been —" I stopped then as a fearful possibility struck me. "The children? Lally and Nora, they are — nothing is wrong?"

"Not at all, Miss Montrose. They're sleeping like angels, with the watchful Rosalba at their bedside. I did not mean to imply you were remiss in your duties. I went up earlier to discuss an idea with you and was surprised to be told you were out for the evening."

I had regained some of my composure now and was relieved that everything was as it should be. So I could ask more calmly, "And that is? Your idea, sir?" I hoped to bypass any explanation about where I had been and with whom. But

Randall was not that easily diverted.

"It is something we can take up at another time," he said brusquely and walked along with me toward the doors leading inside, holding one open for me.

"And did you have a pleasurable evening?" he asked.

In a way, his curiosity rather amused me.

We walked through the foyer and, at the stairway leading to the second floor, I paused. One hand resting on the broad marble balustrade, I replied, "Yes, very," then added, "I hope yours was pleasant, as well."

Randall's dark eyes flashed, and I saw the tensing of his strong jaw. At the same time I could not help thinking how splendid he looked in his evening clothes.

"Well, it wasn't!" he retorted. "Another evening of twiddle-twaddle, inane gossip, and shallow conversation!"

"I'm sorry to hear that."

"Well, it's no concern of yours. No more than what you do with your free time is mine," he growled.

His vehemence surprised me. I was under the impression that the social whirl was something he thoroughly relished. In fact, his reply so astonished me that I blurted out the next thought that came into my head. "I'm sorry . . . especially since I have just had the most remarkable experience. I have just seen the Colosseum by moonlight."

Randall's frown only deepened. "Not alone, I assume, not by the bedazzled expression on your face. I suppose you saw it with that Italian tutor I was foolish enough to engage."

My indignation rose as quickly as the color stained my cheeks. But I drew myself up in my most dignified manner and replied coolly, "If there is nothing else you wish to discuss, I'll say good night."

Immediately Randall's attitude changed. "I beg your pardon, Miss Montrose. My remark was entirely uncalled-for. My apology. I repeat, your private life is your own, and it was out of line to question it in any way." He stepped forward, then halted. "I am in your debt for the excellent way you have taken over the care of Nora and Lally. You are very important to them and —" He hesitated before adding — "and to me."

With a slight bow, he said, "Good night, Miss Montrose," and walked in the direction of the grand salon, leaving me both shaken and bewildered.

chapter
13

In the weeks that followed that incident, it seemed that Randall's attitude toward me changed subtly. He was pleasant and much less moody when he visited our wing of the villa, and he stayed longer, showing an interest in the girls' progress to an extent I had not noticed before. He asked questions, not always directly concerned with the children — questions about my own childhood, my education at Cameron Hall. He seemed especially interested in those phases of my upbringing that dealt with the traditional training of a Southern lady.

While I found myself intrigued by his complex personality, I realized again that such fascination held danger. Sometimes, lulled by a rare glimpse of a gentler side, I would entertain a fantasy that our relationship could be something more than employer and employee. Then, just as suddenly, there would be that flash of lightning-quick temper, his mood as dark as storm clouds, and any hope I had of knowing what lay beneath the surface of the man vanished.

I never allowed myself to fantasize long, however, never asked myself the question that hovered in my heart.

To be realistic about any foolish thoughts about Randall, I had only to observe what was going on around me. The Elliotts were very much in evidence that spring. Invitations flowed between the two villas.

Whenever Peggy and her formidable mother were visiting, Randall always brought them, either to the schoolroom or out to the garden where I was with the children. It was here I could see clearly the net the beautiful young woman and her mother were weaving about Randall.

I tried to be reserved but pleasant, all the while seething inside over their condescending manner toward me. I noticed Randall did not enter in to their conversation with Nora and Lally, just stood there a little apart, smiling to himself. Could not he see what they were doing? Trying to win the hearts of these innocent little things, pretending an interest in what they were saying? It infuriated me even as I chastised myself for being critical.

One such day, watching a performance by the Elliotts of such proportion it could have almost been a satirical play, I happened to glance at Randall. Was I mistaken, or did his eyelid close in a furtive wink when he caught my eye?

Of course, I could not be sure. But from that moment I began to suspect that the Elliotts' motives might be more transparent to him than I had at first imagined.

Still, the morning horseback rides continued, as well as the afternoon sightseeing tours, the teas, the dinners, the fêtes and opera-going. Whether he enjoyed it all or not — as he had indicated that night when he met me coming home from the Colosseum — he continued to go.

In the meantime, my friendship with Pietro developed and deepened. It became a very special kind of bond. In our walks and talks I had learned more of his family background, and how even though their politics were sharply opposed, Pietro loved his father and missed the close family ties. Poverty was new to him, and I empathized with his struggles, having known it first-hand myself.

We had much in common and delighted in the things we shared, never mentioning the wide differences that separated us.

Pietro was an incomparable companion. His English was nearly flawless, for he had studied it at the University and, since I needed practice in Italian, we conversed in both languages. He had a love of art and a knowledge about the famous painters, their works and their lives. To visit a gallery with him was an unforgettable experience. Since the girls took naps or rested during the hottest part of the day, I often took that time to go with Pietro to some of the places they would not have particularly enjoyed.

Soon it became a weekly outing for the two of us. My memories of Rome are all linked to those afternoons — strolling in the Borghese Gardens, climbing the Spanish Steps to visit the golden church with its double towers, tossing coins into the magnificent Trevi Fountain, and laughing with the crowd as the little boys jumped in searching for them while watchful constables gave chase.

Pietro loved music, like all Italians. Of course, he could not afford to go to the opera now, but he would tell me the plots of all Verdi's great ones and hum the arias. Whatever we did together was complete enjoyment.

When the summer heat became intense,

Randall announced we would spend the next six weeks in Switzerland. I was always amazed at how rich people have all the details of traveling arranged for them. They merely decide and everything is taken care of — the train reservations, the packing, the managing of all the small annoyances of moving from one residence to another. The actual transportation is carried out with greatest ease and comfort.

Soon we were in a first-class compartment moving along the breathtaking vistas of the Italian Alps, then finally merging into the fairy-tale land of crystal lakes, the sheer beauty of glistening snow-peaked mountains, flower-filled meadows, cerulean blue skies.

When I had told Pietro we would be gone for over a month, he seemed upset. It was the first time since our midnight viewing of the Colosseum that he took my hand, covered it with kisses, and then said, "I shall miss you very much, *cara mia,* I will be lost without you."

When I tried to withdraw my hand, he clasped it firmly, looked deeply into my eyes, and spoke in his soft, musical voice. "Have you ever wondered, Dru, why you came to Italy? Why we happened to meet? Have you not a clear vision of destiny?"

In Switzerland, I had time to think of Pietro and where our closeness might be leading. Should I, when we returned to Italy, break off the relationship? By now the little girls were speaking fluent Italian, chatting freely with Rosalba constantly. There was really no need for Pietro's lessons anymore. I should inform Randall of this, but, for selfish reasons, I was reluctant to do so. If Pietro were no longer in my life, I would be very lonely. But was it fair to continue, seeding hope in Pietro's heart that there could be more between us than friendship?

I did not dream how quickly my whole dilemma would be resolved and in a way I could never have imagined.

In Switzerland, we stayed at a chateau with painted shutters and sculptured balconies. The little girls and I slept in high, recessed beds with feather mattresses and downy comforters. We hiked winding mountain trails, breathed deeply of pristine air, ate heartily of the rich cheeses, creamy goat's milk and fresh-baked bread. Nora and Lally grew rosy-cheeked and plump in the healthfully cool Swiss climate.

When Randall went mountain-climbing with some English and American gentlemen and their guide, and was gone for three days, I lay awake those nights, wondering what I would do should anything happen to the girls' father. For the first time, I realized the depth of my commitment to my little cousins, how much I loved them. And for the first time, I allowed myself to think what I would do, how that relationship with them would be altered if Randall remarried. More to the point, and I shuddered at the thought, what would I do if Randall married *Peggy Elliott?!*

The first Thursday we were back at the villa and Pietro came for our lessons, I felt that a momentous declaration was imminent. His eyes were shining suspiciously when he arrived that morning with little silk painted fans for Nora and Lally, a lovely bouquet of flowers for me.

"Welcome back!" he said smiling, his eyes caressing me openly.

Somehow I got through our lesson that day, but all the time there was a nervous anticipation, a premonition perhaps.

After Pietro dismissed the children and they ran into the garden, he gathered up his textbooks. "Walk with me to the gate,

167

Dru." There was a plea in his voice I could not refuse.

I will never forget how beautiful the garden was that day. The sun, sifting through the towering cypresses that lined the road to the gate, cast blue-violet shadows. Oleander bushes in full bloom were bursts of flame against the green foliage.

As we walked, Pietro reached for my hand and captured it in his. "I have missed you desperately, Dru. The days were so long, the nights endless while you were away. I know I have no right to speak. I am, at the present, without means, without anything to offer . . . but my heart. And this I do with my whole soul."

He stopped abruptly and swung me around to face him. Holding my hand in both of his, he pressed it against his chest. I could feel the erratic pounding of his heart, fluttering as wildly as my own.

"Marry me, *cara mia*. I love you so dearly. We could find such happiness, for what more do two people need?"

He pulled me closer, murmuring endearments in Italian. His questions raced through my mind. Was Pietro right in his gentle insistence that we were destined for each other?

Pietro was looking at me with such

tender ardor I felt my head spin. What would it be like to live always in Italy, this country of enchantment? I had come to love it, to revel in its ancient beauty, its color, its culture, its warm and beautiful people.

This charming young man wanted me to marry him. He was saying loving, persuasive things and I was only half-listening, my own thoughts in excited turmoil. He made it all sound so natural, so possible, so simple. And yet something told me it was not simple. Not simple at all.

There were wide disparities between us — differences of nationality, background, religion, personality. Could all these be bridged by love?

Now Pietro had drawn me into his arms. I looked up into his sensitive face, the aquiline features, the curve of his mouth, then I felt the warmth of his lips on mine. And, for a moment, I could not think at all.

The sound of the gates opening, followed by the slapping of reins and the scattering of gravel beneath carriage wheels, alerted us to its approach, and we broke apart . . . but not before I had caught a glimpse of Randall Bondurant, his implacable face turned to us as he passed.

"I must go, Pietro," I said breathlessly.

"*Cara*, please consider all that I have said," he begged before he kissed my hand again in parting.

I have always found when I paint that I can think of nothing else but the colors I choose, the problem of the picture I am trying to portray. That afternoon, with my mind in a frenzy, I decided to take my little easel and paintbox out to the garden and thus free myself of the perplexing anxieties Pietro's proposal had caused.

Nora, too, had shown a definite talent for art, so I thought this might be a good time to instruct her, thus further occupying my thoughts and attention. However, she soon lost patience when her attempts did not suit her, and went off with Lally down to the lily pond to play with her dolls.

Left alone, I concentrated on my project. It should be a picture of the villa, I decided. If it turned out well, I would have it matted and framed for Mama.

The rays of the late afternoon sun shed a lovely golden haze on the house, intensifying the orange of the stucco, accenting the touches of gleaming white marble. The surrounding trees cast dramatic shadows. I became excited at the possibilities. Quickly I mixed a deep blue with red and brushed in purple strokes to indicate the delicate tracery of the leaves against the stucco walls.

I was so completely engrossed in my painting that I didn't hear Rosalba right away. When I glanced up, she was hurrying across the velvet lawn, calling my name.

"Signorina Dru!" She waved her apron like a flag.

She seemed agitated, her big, black eyes wide, her olive skin rosy with exertion. "Oh, Signorina, you must go at once. Signor Bondurant wishes you to come to his study. I will stay with the bambinas. You go!" She stopped for breath, flattening one hand against her breast.

I started to clean my brushes, wipe my hands on my paint rag when Rosalba said, "I think you better go at once, Signorina. The signor seems in a temper!"

I looked at her, frowning. It was unusual for the cheerful Rosalba to be upset. Something about Randall's order had bothered her.

The thought struck me that Randall might have come to some snap assumption earlier when he had seen me and Pietro together. Was it possible that, even before the carriage had rolled through the gates, he had seen our embrace? Perhaps I was being called in for a reprimand, or even worse, for dismissal!

I felt a cold finger of fear rippling down my spine. Leaving my things where they were, I started across the lawn toward the house.

chapter
14

Once inside the villa, I paused briefly in front of the baroque mirror to remove the wide-brimmed straw hat I'd worn to shade my eyes while I painted.

I frowned at my reflection. I had grown careless about protecting my complexion from the Italian sun, and I noted the apricot glow of my skin, flushed with hurrying. Oh, well, there was nothing to be done about that, I sighed, smoothing back my hair. If the Signor was as impatient as Rosalba had indicated, there was no time.

I skimmed up the marble stairway to the second floor and along the corridor to Randall's study. Outside the tall, carved double doors, I lifted my hand to knock, then hesitated, bracing myself for the encounter to come. Then I rapped firmly.

"Come," came a resonant summons.

Randall was standing at the floor-length windows that opened out onto the terrace, his back to me as I entered.

"You wanted to see me, sir?"

"Yes, Miss Montrose." Randall turned slowly to face me. I was struck again by the sculptured strength of his features and saw in them a decided likeness to the statues of ancient Romans I had studied — the same high-bridged nose, the same bold jawline. "Please, sit down. I have something of great importance to discuss with you." He gestured to one of the chairs.

I took a seat and waited for him to speak.

He clasped his hands behind his back and began pacing. "First, I want to say that in the year and a half you have been engaged as my daughters' governess, I have been most pleased with their progress and development. Not only in their lessons, in which there has been marked improvement, but also in their spirits and health. From this, I can only surmise that your care and supervision is responsible. They are becoming the happy, healthy children I longed for them to be."

"Thank you," I murmured, surprised by his unexpected compliment.

Abruptly he stopped striding back and forth and stood surveying me for what seemed a full moment before going on. "Furthermore, they seem to be acquiring

174

the graceful manners I always admired in Southern ladies. I can assume this is also due to their exposure to one of your . . . gentle breeding." I could feel the heat mounting once more to my face. I was accustomed to lavish compliments only from Pietro. "It has ever been my desire for them to grow up confident of their position, able to take their place in society — that society to which their heritage entitles them."

He paused, still riveting me with his penetrating eyes, and I waited, my breath caught in my throat. "It is my concern that my daughters should be prepared for the life they will live as young ladies. Consequently, they must acquire the social skills expected of their station. This kind of training requires a special person . . . so in the future there shall be no need of a governess."

At his words, I felt a tight, clutching sensation in my stomach. So, this was not to be the reprimand I feared. It was going to be worse — a dismissal — and for an instant, I recalled the downfall of the dour-faced Miss Ogilvie and empathized with her humiliation.

Because of the sudden roaring in my ears, I missed Mr. Bondurant's next words.

My mind raced headlong into my immediate future. What was I to do? Wealthy Italians paid *well* for English or American governesses, I had heard, but treated them shabbily. Perhaps it would not be too late to reapply for a position at Thornycroft, though the idea galled.

The sound of Randall's voice broke into my rambling thoughts. "So . . . as their father, I have been giving some thoughtful consideration as to what is the best for my daughters' future and have decided quite definitely that they must be in their own country. I have seen enough of impoverished noblemen seeking rich American heiresses. Well . . . never mind about that . . . I won't have it for my daughters." He had resumed his pacing by this time and was intent on communicating something very important to me . . . but where was it leading?

"No, what they need is a real home where they can meet and entertain a variety of suitors from among the finest families of Virginia. For this, they need *two* parents — especially a mother skilled in the social graces. She must be a lady of cultured taste, of refinement and impeccable family. In other words, I have decided to remarry and provide my daughters with an acceptable stepmother."

His statement did not come as much of a shock. I knew, of course, that Randall Bondurant had an active social life. His remarriage someday was almost a foregone conclusion from the beginning.

What shocked me was my reaction to this announcement. An immediate indefinable sense of loss rushed over me, and I felt quite faint.

"Perhaps I am putting this badly —" he said, no doubt noting my stricken look.

"Oh, no, sir. I understand perfectly. When would you like me to leave? Or do you plan for me to accompany the girls back to England or even to the States?"

He whirled around, eyes flashing, color mounting into the lean handsome face. "Leave? Did I say anything about your leaving?"

"But, sir, I thought —"

"I said there was no further need for a governess, that now there was need for a *mother* — *a wjfe!* Druscilla, I am asking *you* to be that person — to assume the position, in fact, that you have been in essence since you became the girls' governess. You are ideally qualified. What's more, they love you and would be devastated to lose you." His voice modulated, and he turned an inquiring gaze on me. "Miss Montrose — Druscilla — I want you to marry me, become my wife and stepmother to the children."

I don't think I gasped aloud, although my true reaction warranted such surprise. His words left me totally incapable of speech.

Randall, on the other hand, had not seemed to notice my stunned silence. He went on pacing, talking as he did so, oblivious to my bewilderment.

"Of course, I realize you may want some time to think this over, although, I cannot really imagine what objections you could possibly have to such an arrangement. It is ideal for everyone concerned." He paused and directed his next words as if expecting me to argue.

"Am I right in assuming that you have no other source of income except the salary I pay you? And that you send half of that home to help support your mother? You have no other marriage prospects at present, no romantic attachments?"

Wildly I thought of Pietro. I almost started to name him, since Randall was so confident, almost arrogantly so, that I would accept his offer gratefully. But he wasn't through with his monologue.

"I perceive you to be an intelligent, practical young woman. With this marriage, you will be comfortably settled for life. I can assure you that everything will be drawn up legally. It is a European custom to sign a marriage contract in which everything is clearly defined beforehand. Each party knows exactly what is expected and what to expect in return."

I felt the blood drain from my cheeks, and I thought surely I would faint, though I had never done such a thing in my life.

"Your life with the girls will go on unchanged in the main, except that you will have more authority to make decisions for them without consulting me — if I should be away.

"Besides that, you will have a generous allowance for clothes and other expenses as befits your position as my wife. This will be completely yours to use at your discretion, and will be separate from any inheritance coming to my daughters at my death. You will, as my wife, be beneficiary to my estate as is usual in any marriage."

I still could not find words to speak. He gave me a sharp glance. Then, as if to meet any possible objection I might have, he hurried on. "To put your mind at ease, in case you had any misgivings otherwise, I intend to include in the document that I will make no demands of any kind on your person, your privacy. I waive any conjugal rights. You will be my wife in name only, but with all the privileges of the position in the eyes of the law. If such an agreement seems equitable and fair to you, I can offer you a life of affluence, interesting travel, even luxury, if you will — something I realize your family has not known in their reduced circumstances."

Slowly the full impact of what he was suggesting began to penetrate my stunned consciousness. Marriage to Randall Bondurant would be a business contract with rules, benefits, and obligations to be mutually upheld and officially documented. What a clever and calculated plan, I thought, to provide Bondurant's children with the best of care — a kind of security bond.

Not a shred of emotion was visible in Bondurant's voice or expression. He might be arguing the merits of any other business transaction. He seemed assured I should find the arrangement completely satisfactory.

For a moment, I let myself think of Pietro — his soft voice, his warm, dark eyes, his love of music and art and poetry and me! How differently he would have spoken to me of marriage.

I could almost hear Pietro saying, "We are destined for each other, Dru. Why else would God have brought us to this time and place in all eternity if not that we were meant for each other?"

"Well?" Bondurant's voice roughened with impatience.

I came back to the demanding present with a little start. Clasping my hands tightly together to stop their trembling, I gathered my composure enough to reply, "Sir, I must confess this comes as — as a somewhat surprising — proposal. And indeed, I would like — that is — I need time, to consider, to —"

"Yes, yes, of course. Take some time!" he interrupted.

Thus dismissed, I started for the door. My hand was poised above the doorknob when his voice followed me sharply.

"I trust you will not take . . . too long . . . to give me your answer."

Outside the study door, I drew a long shaky breath. My heart was beating so hard and so fast that I put my hand on my breast as if to still its pounding.

I almost ran up the next flight of steps to my own room, and once behind the relative safety of the closed door gave way to uncontrollable shaking.

Had I understood him correctly? Was Randall Bondurant really asking me to become his wife?

chapter
15

I went to the dressing table and, with trembling hands, lifted the bottle of eau de cologne, soaked my handkerchief with it, and pressed the damp cloth to my burning face and temples.

I had been completely unprepared for the scenario that had just taken place. Randall must have been considering this proposition for some time, or he would not have had all the details so thoroughly outlined. Had such an arrangement been in his mind weeks ago, even a month ago?

I recalled an incident in Switzerland. We had taken the children to a playground in the center of town and were sitting on a bench nearby as Lally and Nora rode the carousel. Each time they sailed by on their wooden horses, they would wave and call, "Look, Drucie!"

Over and over, round and round. Each time, I responded, "Yes, darling, I see!" After at least a dozen turns, I realized

Randall was observing me.

When I glanced at him, he remarked, "You really love the children, don't you?"

Surprised, I had replied, "Why of course I love them! They're my own flesh and blood."

Now, I wondered if Randall had been testing me, making some kind of comparison with the other females of his acquaintance.

I walked over to the tall windows, opened them, and stepped out onto the balcony. The sky was a hyacinth blue as early evening descended into the garden. From the next room I could hear the voices of the children as Rosalba helped them with their baths. My heart contracted, and I knew more surely than ever what Nora and Lally meant to me, how impossible it would be for me ever to give them up.

But what about my feelings for Randall Bondurant? They had been suppressed so long it was difficult to be honest even with myself. My initial girlish attraction to him at the time of Alair's wedding had lain dormant all these years. Now, even though I knew him to be a man of moods and of sudden, bewildering tempers, I also knew him to be a tender, loving father.

In my heart of hearts, I knew I had become as much entwined in Randall's life as in those of his children. I could not imagine life without any of them.

But what of love — romantic love — such as Pietro offered me? I was, after all, only twenty-two. Could I exist in the hope that Randall might one day love me? If he had truly loved Alair, so different in every way from me, it would be folly to hope that such a thing could happen.

No, if I were going to accept Randall's proposal, it must be on his terms.

"Marriage is an honorable estate, not to be entered into lightly, inadvisedly —" From somewhere, the words of the marriage ceremony repeated themselves in my brain.

Was our mutual love for the children enough of a bond for marriage? Was it a valid reason to forego the chance that I might know love to its fullest with some other man later on? So many things to consider, so many conflicting feelings! I wished for someone to consult, some trusted friend to advise me.

Then I realized that I was overlooking the obvious. I had always been taught to pray over decisions, and this was surely the most important I had yet been called upon to make. Leafing through my Bible, I searched the Psalms and read at random in Proverbs.

Finally, I buried my head in my hands and simply told God what was in my heart: "Lord, show me what to do. I want to please You. Is it Your will that I become stepmother to Lally and Nora? Will You give me some kind of assurance that this is Your plan for me?"

I stayed there on my knees for some time. The only thing that came to me was the familiar verse: "Suffer the little children to come unto Me, and forbid them not, for of such is the kingdom of heaven."

It was such a spontaneous thought that I did not trust it. I remembered Auntie Kate saying once that any decision that was not life or death could wait three days to be made. In that time God would do one of three things: He would check you clearly, He would change the circumstances, or He would give peace about the matter.

Three days, I thought. I'll wait three days and then I'll pray again. When I got up from my knees, all the troubled confusion I'd felt earlier had left. At least I knew *that* had been the right decision.

A gentle knock at my door and Rosalba's soft voice reminded me, "Miss Dru, the children are waiting for you to join them for supper."

"I'm coming, Rosalba," I called and hurriedly checked my face and hair in the mirror for traces of my emotional turmoil. Then, I hurried out and went to the playroom, where supper had been set out.

Later, when each child hugged and kissed me good night, it seemed the confirmation I'd been seeking.

"I love you, Drucie!" Two little hearts echoed their love. I felt a lump rise in my throat as the little arms held me tight, and my eyes misted over as I tucked them in for the night.

Three days later I stood again outside Randall's study door, awaiting his call to enter.

He was sitting at the ornate, curved table he used for a desk and raised his head as I came in, a frown on his face.

At my approach, he got to his feet. "So, have you reached your decision then." Was it my own nervousness or did *he* seem uncertain? He picked up the silver dagger-shaped letter opener and turned it over several times in his open palm.

I took a deep breath and nodded. "Yes, I have."

"And?" His dark eyebrows lifted.

With greater serenity than I felt, I spoke. "I have considered all the things you said, thought it over seriously — and prayed."

"It has taken you long enough," Randall interrupted briskly, walking over to the inlaid side table where a decanter of wine stood on a silver tray beside delicate tulip-shaped glasses. His long fingers toyed with the domed top. "So then?" he prompted me.

"I love the girls with all my heart. Leaving them is —"

"Leaving them?" he echoed harshly.

"I was about to say that leaving them is unthinkable. Furthermore, I must think of my mother. What you have proposed would provide me with the security —"

"Security? There is no security on earth, only opportunity. My proposal would give you the *opportunity* to do whatever you wished." Scorn seemed to narrow his eyes as his glance grazed me. He very deliberately poured a reddish liquid into one of the glasses, raised it to his lips, then asked bluntly, "Are you telling me you have decided to grasp this *opportunity?*"

Color rushed into my face. I could even feel my ears tingle with warmth. Put that way, it sounded so crass, so mercenary. I felt rebuffed, uncomfortable, gauche.

Immediately, Randall's expression underwent a distinct change. "I apologize, my dear. I didn't intend to hurt you. It is just that I have heard too many fools make too many casual remarks about security to be able to swallow pat phrases. I, personally, know that life is full of risk as well as opportunity. As Shakespeare said, 'There is a tide in the affairs of men, which taken at the flood, leads on to fortune.' So many people fail to realize when their own tide is at the flood. I hope you are not among them."

I clasped my hands tightly behind me and lifted my chin in what I hoped was a display of Montrose pride and dignity. "I mean, sir, that I am prepared to accept your offer of marriage."

"Fine!" Randall said heartily. He held up his glass. "I toast your sensibility. I will go ahead then with all the arrangements."

Plans moved forward rapidly. The children were told and reacted with a joyfulness that touched me deeply. They smothered me with hugs and kisses.

"Now you will be with us always, Drucie!" Nora declared ecstatically while Lally squeezed me so tightly I could scarcely breathe.

But as the actual wedding day neared, I was filled with misgivings. Even then I was too busy to dwell too much upon them. There was much to be done before we returned to America, to Virginia — the most difficult being breaking the news to Pietro of my impending marriage.

It was an emotional moment. The distress he felt showed in his dark, sorrowful eyes.

"But, cara Dru, it is you and I who were destined for each other!" he protested.

I tried to explain my reasons, but they seemed shallow and grasping instead of devoted and selfless.

Pietro shook his head sadly. "I know I had nothing to offer you — not wealth nor position. If we had met at another time, perhaps — but —" He shrugged helplessly.

"I will always think of you with great affection, Pietro. You have made my time in Rome very special."

"And you, *cara mia,* will remain always in my heart." He bowed over my hand, kissing it for the last time. *"Arivederci."*

I watched him go down the garden path, disappear in the shadow of the silvery cypress trees. I felt a strange urge to call him back, but it was too late. I had already charted my destiny.

How many times in the days that followed did I think of the adage I had heard over and over in my childhood: "You can have what you want if you're willing to pay the price. But never forget the price must be paid, and sometimes it is more than you bargained for."

This was brought sharply to my mind the day of our wedding. Even though I was superbly gowned by one of the leading salons of Rome at Randall's insistence, I felt as forlorn as any waif as I dressed that morning.

"Oh, Signorina, you look bella!" sighed Rosalba as she assisted me with the many buttons.

My dress, a rose-ivory moire silk, was more elegant than anything I had ever owned. It was fashioned in the latest style, a fitted basque trimmed with ecru lace as was the overskirt which was drawn back into a bustle, the skirt descending in tiers of lace ruffles. My bonnet was of Tuscan straw, adorned with ivory velvet roses and grosgrain streamers. I wore creamy kid gloves. The only part of the ceremony that I remember clearly was my struggle to unbutton the left one to free my finger to receive the narrow gold band Randall slipped on it.

Since neither of us was Catholic, we could not arrange to be married in *any* of the dozens of Catholic churches in Rome. And the minister of the Anglican church to which I had taken the girls several times was in England on leave. So we settled for the impersonal, civil pronouncement administered by an Italian government official. It was hardly any girl's dream. For me, to take this most important step of my life, so far from home and family, seemed almost sacrilegious.

I had not anticipated the sense of letdown nor the feeling of depression that followed the brief ceremony.

As we stepped out of the dim interior of the building into the dazzling noon sunlight of the square, I saw two old Italian women tending a flower stand.

They looked at me curiously as we passed. I wondered what they were thinking as they put their heads together. What were they saying? "How grave the bridegroom looks? How pale and serious the bride?" Were they lamenting a wedding without music or flowers, the scent of burning candles, no family or friends throwing rose petals, calling felicitations and greetings?

Well, what had I expected? I asked myself as we got back into the carriage for our return to the villa. I had settled for a marriage of mutual benefit. It was merely a contract we had both signed. Nothing had been said about love.

And yet, nonetheless, love had been the basis — love for the children, love for my mother, and my undeclared, unreturned love for Randall.

Since I had agreed to the terms, why did I feel such a devastating emptiness about it all? I pondered this question on the silent ride home.

Only the children prevented the day from being a dismal disaster. They came running down the terrace steps to meet us, followed by a beaming Rosalba.

I bent to embrace them, gathering them close, responding to their innocent, unconditional love. This was the reason for my decision, I reminded myself, and their happiness was worth it all!

I felt Randall's eyes upon us and looked up at him, but he turned quickly away, saying to Rosalba, "We'll have our lunch on the piazza today." Then he went striding up the steps ahead of us.

It was a festive meal. The cook had taken special pains with each dish. There was champagne and fresh peaches and a wedding cake. The children were happy and talkative, a welcome distraction from Randall's extraordinary taciturnity.

Occasionally, I glanced over at him and inadvertently met his gaze. It seemed particularly expressionless. I found myself wishing desperately that the circumstances were different and that Randall's eyes held the kind of light I had once seen in them when he looked at Alair.

Quickly, I reminded myself of the "arrangement" that precluded that possibility. But very humanly I could not help hoping that one day — maybe far in the future — the admiration and respect Randall had expressed for me might grow into love.

After the day filled with unusual excitement and tension, I felt quite weary. I put the girls to bed as usual and went to my room. Although exhausted, I was not sleepy. I opened the windows and stepped out onto the balcony.

It was an enchanted evening — soft blue twilight deepening into purple. One by one, the stars came out. Later, a pale thumbnail of a moon appeared above the line of cypresses.

A kind of melancholy welled up within that I was spending my wedding night alone, with no one to share this beauty.

It was then I saw the tall, solitary figure walking along the garden path. I recognized it at once.

Had Randall, too, found sleep difficult on this, our wedding night? I had never known him to walk alone in the garden at night. Usually he would be out with friends. Did he no longer feel free to do so now that we were married? Perhaps he was even now regretting our contract. Did I?

As I watched him disappear into the maze near the fountain, the question begged an answer. Was marrying Randall Bondurant really my destiny, or would this marriage ultimately mean my destruction?

Part III
September 1884

chapter
16

September 1884

Dearest Mama,

By the time you receive this letter, we will probably be in England ready to set sail for America, for home. But while it is still all fresh in my mind, I wanted to tell you about our "wedding trip" — if you can call traveling with two children, our Italian maid, and numerous pieces of luggage, dolls, and toys — a wedding trip!

Randall wanted to visit Germany and Austria before we leave Europe. He has had a long-standing invitation to visit a friend, an Austrian nobleman, and stay at his hunting lodge near the famous Black Forest.

It is mysteriously beautiful country, deserving of its name. Dense rows of tall, silver firs with the light barely filtering through make it seem almost eerie. Nora declared it looked like just such a forest as Hansel and Gretel wandered in until they came upon the witch's cottage. Lally moved closer to me at this.

The lodge belonging to Herr Hesse was a large, dark-timbered structure with a heavy overhanging roof. Set in the midst of this shadowy valley surrounded by the looming mountains, it was a bit foreboding. The interior was gloomy, as well, with its vaulted ceilings and shuttered windows.

In the morning the men went hunting. At noon, we women and children followed by carriage to a pine-needled clearing for a picnic. A "picnic" there is hardly the casual affair that we enjoy in Mayfield. Long before we arrived, servants had set up long banquet tables, covered with damask cloths, and had brought out hampers of lobster salad, salmon mousse, venison, delicious varieties of fresh fruits — plums, pears, and luscious grapes — chilled beverages and hot coffee. It was a feast fit for royalty.

From there, we drove to Vienna — a city of squares, palaces, grand buildings, lovely parks, and delectable pastries. Randall asked me if I wanted to go to the opera, but I declined. There is no lack of music throughout the city — a quartet playing continually in the lobby of our hotel, a band in the park where we took the children every day, and strolling musicians in every coffeehouse and wine garden. Vienna is a city of make-believe. Every scene seems the setting for a romantic tableau.

The boat trip down the Rhine was for me the most enjoyable part of the whole trip. On either side steep cliffs ascended to green meadows; picturesque castles perched on craggy heights. One's imagination takes wings, picturing brave knights baffling dragons on the steep mountain passes to rescue fair damsels. You may be sure the girls and I exchanged story ideas of princesses locked in high towers, awaiting the arrival of the handsome prince.

In Berlin, we put Rosalba on the train to Rome before we boarded our own train for Paris. The parting was tearful, but promises were made to return to Italy one day.

Sad as I was to leave dear Rosalba, who had been such a help and comfort to me with the children, I was looking forward to my first trip to France.

I will tell you in person about our visits to the Louvre, Versailles, Mont St. Michel and the Cathedral de Notre Dame — all awe-inspiring, impressive, overwhelming! But I know what would be of greatest interest to you, Mama, was my visit — insisted upon, I must add, by Randall — to the salon of Monsieur Worth.

Accompanied by Randall, I set out early in the morning by carriage from the hotel. It was so early that baker boys were running along the streets with baskets full of freshly baked bread to deliver to the hotels for breakfasts.

An appointment had been made for me, and we were ushered into the establishment of one of the world's most famous designers. There was a hushed atmosphere intensified by the thick carpets, the velvet draperies, the low voices of the modistes and their assistants all dressed in elegant black gowns. I was taken into a mirrored room, helped to undress, and had my measurements taken so that any of the models we chose could be made up to my exact proportions.

I heard Randall telling the head modiste that three of the outfits must be ready by the time we left for England; anything else I chose could be sent to use later in Virginia.

Of course, I was thrilled to have designer ensembles made to order for me. However, I did rather resent the hours of fitting required while Randall took the children to

Les Bois and then on a boat ride down the Seine while I was trapped in one of the dressing rooms at Worth's, being pinned and tucked.

The final result, however, was well *"worth"* it. Wait until you see my traveling outfit! The softest of cashmere wool, with cinnamon velvet trim, the jacket collar and cuffs of pale mink; an afternoon tea gown of rich velvet, edged in satin and point lace, and a ball gown of gossamer tulle, embroidered with seed pearls. I can just see your expression when you see your daughter in her Parisian finery!

After an amazingly smooth Channel crossing, we took the train up to London. The English countryside is like turning the pages of a picture book — green hedges, flocks of peacefully grazing sheep, stone cottages nestled in rolling hills, here and there a church steeple.

Then we rushed into the huge tunnel of Victoria Station. From there, a carriage ride through crowded, noisy, dirty streets to the Claridge Hotel, which is all elegance and splendor. Footmen, I guess you call them, in powdered wigs, scarlet and gold jackets, white stockings, and buckled shoes took care of our luggage.

Our rooms are luxurious — huge bouquets of flowers in vases, fires in the fireplaces, rosy-cheeked maids bringing hot water for baths.

The children were so tired that they fell asleep the instant their heads touched the pillows. Since Randall had suggested that he and I dine downstairs in the dining room, we arranged with the management for a maid to stay with the girls in our suite while we were out.

I must get ready, dear Mama, but I will see you soon to regale you in person with other stories of our travels.

In two days time, we sail for America, then come by train to Richmond. I can scarcely wait to set foot on Virginia soil again and to see my dearest mother after so long a time!

Ever your loving daughter,
Druscilla Montrose Bondurant

I ended my letter to Mama, then went to bathe and dress for dinner. In the six weeks we had been traveling, Randall and I had never been alone for a moment. Except for the stilted morning of our wedding ceremony in Rome, we either had the children with us or the servants or friends.

I felt a little nervous spending a dinner hour alone with him. What would we find to talk about? Would it be stiff and awkward and uncomfortable?

Well, we were married now, weren't we? I'd have to get used to that fact. I must remember all Auntie Kate's and Mama's training on poise, proper manners, and lady-like behavior, especially since my deportment had been one of the factors in Randall's proposal. I mustn't disappoint him!

I had not worn the lovely dinner gown from Worth's since my final fitting, so Randall had never seen me in it.

Now, as I took it out from its tissue wrappings, I drew a long breath. It was exquisite! Of pale blue grenadine, scalloped in peacock blue velvet, its overskirt was draped in back and fell in cascading ruffles into a short train.

After I had put it on and buttoned the dozen tiny covered buttons on the tightly fitted basque, I could not believe my own eyes. Who was that tall, elegant woman looking back at me in the mirror?

I felt a giggle bubble up inside and held my hand over my mouth as I preened in front of the looking glass, back and front, both sides, giving my train a little kick as I turned. Who would ever have dreamed that Dru Montrose of Mayfield, Virginia, would be dressed by Worth and dining in one of the most exclusive hotels in London?

My hair, still damp from my bath, went smoothly into a chignon. This simple style suited me so much better than the fussy ones in vogue.

Then I slipped in my sapphire and pearl earrings, picked up my fan and small evening bag, and went to meet my . . . husband. The idea was still foreign to me. I hoped my appearance would please him.

He was waiting for me at the foot of the carpeted stairway of the lobby and escorted me into the dining room.

Everything was perfection — the soft music playing throughout the meal, the tables with their smooth white linen, fresh flowers in crystal vases, the rich, delicious food, superbly served.

Much to my surprise, for I had feared we would have nothing to say to each other without the children, our conversation went well. It was filled with observations about our travels, the sights, the people, the places and events we had experienced together, but with different impressions. We even laughed about some of the incidents that, in retrospect, seemed humorous to us now.

Our after-dinner coffee was served in tiny, egg-shell thin cups. Regretfully, I realized this pleasant evening was drawing to a close. Over the rim of my cup, I searched Randall's face, hoping to find a similar reluctance to leave. But his expression was unreadable.

Knowing I could delay no longer, I gathered my things and we left. To my surprise, as we passed the ballroom where an orchestra was playing and couples were dancing, Randall paused.

"Would you care to dance?" he asked.

"Yes, very much!" I replied, delighted.

He escorted me into the ballroom and there I moved into his arms as he swept me out onto the floor. So expert a dancer was he, that my feet barely touched the polished surface. We did not speak, simply followed the music, moving together easily as if we had danced together a hundred times before.

As the last strains of the music faded away, we stood only inches apart, our hands still touching. Randall regarded me in a way that both puzzled and stirred me. Then, bowing slightly, he stepped away, offered me his arm again, and we walked back into the lobby.

At the foot of the staircase, Randall said good night. I heard the orchestra striking up another melody and longed to return to that place where spoken words were not necessary.

With the sounds of the lilting music still in my ears, I mounted the stairs to my rooms, feeling the lingering enchantment of the evening. I had been happier in the last hours than I had for a very long time. The subtle tension of the last few weeks seemed to have melted away, and I felt hopeful that my position as Randall's wife might become more than a role I was playing.

Had this evening marked a new beginning, the start of a new relationship for Randall and me?

In two short days, we would sail for America and on to Virginia where we would begin a new life together. Was it possible that the strange destiny that had brought us together promised happiness, after all?

Part IV

Return to Mayfield
1884

Return to Montclair
1885

chapter
17

I found this trans-Atlantic crossing by ship much different from the one I had made a year before. The first time, as the girls' governess, my duties were clearly defined. One express duty had been to keep the children removed from the frantic, festival-like atmosphere of First Class passengers, who considered a trip like this merely an excuse for a two-week party.

This time, Randall had arranged to have a stewardess employed by the steamship company to act as "nanny" to the girls during the trip. Consequently, traveling as Mrs. Bondurant, I would be accorded the untold privileges due Randall's wife.

Dressed in my stylish Worth ensemble with my taupe velvet Paris bonnet, I was led by an obsequious steward down through the carpeted corridors, followed by another, trundling my steamer trunk filled with my new clothes to my deck-side cabin.

He opened the door for me and I stepped into a luxurious room unlike the more compact one I had occupied during our first trip.

Without the constant charge of the children, I was introduced to the many pleasurable occupations afforded passengers on the ship, which was like a floating hotel or resort.

Without meaning to be vain, for I credit all this mainly to my new wardrobe and the fact that I was young, energetic and not at all seasick, I soon had gathered about myself a group of fellow passengers who seemed eager for my company.

I loved being out in the invigorating sea air and enjoyed games of deck-tennis and shuffle board. In the evenings there was always entertainment — theatricals and dancing — which I enjoyed enormously.

I was teased about my Southern accent, but since it was considered "charming," I was not at all disturbed. I loved playing charades and learning the folk dancing being taught. In fact, perhaps for the first time since I had visited the Merediths for that memorable Christmas holiday, I was able to be with people my own age and act accordingly.

Although he did not join in, Randall

seemed tolerant of all my activities. Even though he spent his time playing Bridge and reading on his deck chair, we did walk together twice daily, promenading the deck. And of course, we took our meals together at the table assigned to us.

He was always correctly courteous and solicitous of my welfare, but it was not until midway on our crossing that he introduced matters pertaining to the future.

One day — a day that was somewhat overcast with a brisk wind so that only the hardiest of sailors was out on deck — Randall spoke of our return to Virginia.

"I've been giving a great deal of thought to the house," he said. "It will be the house my daughters grow up in, the house they will be married in, I suppose, when that time comes. I want them to feel the tradition of a home that has passed from generation to generation."

I did not say so, but I thought to myself that Montclair had passed *out* of the family with Randall's acquisition. Then I remembered that by marrying me, the straight line of succession had been re-established. After all, Alair had only been a second cousin, not truly a Montrose.

"So, I have been thinking it should be restored. The wallpaper wasn't the same in

1730 when the house was built, and the wainscoting was unpainted. Am I right?"

I shook my head. "I don't know."

"From the original plans and drawings I've seen, the whole house was done with a simple elegance that was lost somehow in redecorating." He paused, and I knew he was thinking of Alair. Her tastes, a reaction to her extreme poverty, leaned toward extravagance.

"I know all the old furnishings were taken up to the attic and stored there when the new things arrived. Perhaps you could speak to some of the older members of your family, find out from them how the rooms looked. I would like to recreate the original atmosphere of Bon Chance . . . er . . . Montclair," he said. "Do you think you could help me?"

"Oh, yes! I'd like that very much." I was happy that he had suggested the project. It was something we could do together, something that would be sure to draw us closer.

The rest of the voyage was a series of exciting, interesting experiences. Randall seemed to relax and even enjoy himself at some of the evening festivities. The children joined us for luncheon each day and were otherwise happily occupied with the activities planned for the children on board.

The world of shipboard life seemed a life apart from anything I had known, and for those ten days the world outside did not intrude. Even though I was looking forward to my reunion with Mama, I almost hated to see our voyage end.

On the last night at sea, there was a gala ball, where I wore my Paris gown, a fantasy of tulle, lace, and appliqued silk flowers outlined with seed pearls. My dance card was filled by gallant and complimentary partners and then Randall came to claim me for the last dance, after which we formed a giant circle, singing "Auld Lang Syne."

I felt a certain regret, for another carefree episode had come to an end.

In Richmond I got off the train to visit Mama for a few days, and Randall, Nora, and Lally went on to Mayfield.

It was then that the full impact of my marriage on the rest of the family was broken to me.

Mama put it as gently as possible. "I have to be truthful, Dru. Harmony and Clint are very upset about the marriage."

"Why, Mama? Did they think it was too

soon for Randall to marry again? I should think they would be pleased that I am their grandchildren's stepmother. Who could love them more than I?"

Mama shook her head. "I don't think they've thought that far. You have to understand . . . Alair was their only, beloved child. They will never get over her death. They will go on mourning her for the rest of their lives and . . . I suppose . . . they expected Randall to do the same."

"But, life goes on, Mama. Those children need a mother, someone who loves and cares for them as dearly as their own mother would —" I protested.

Mama just looked at me sorrowfully. "That's just the way it is, Dru."

There was a moment of silence, then Mama placed her hand over mine. "Are you happy, Dru? Do you love him?"

I didn't reply right away. I wasn't sure I wanted Mama to know the unusual terms of our marriage. To Mama, love was the only thing that mattered, a love that could last a lifetime, a love that was stronger than death. She would never understand how I could have settled for anything less.

"Yes," I said quietly. But I failed to mention that it was a love that had never been expressed, a love that was not returned.

★ ★ ★

Only a handful of relatives called during the next few days, and then it was time to leave for Mayfield. From the train station I hired a hack to take me out to Bon Chance. As I passed Cameron Hall, I wondered how Auntie Kate and Aunt Garnet and Uncle Rod felt about my marriage to Bondurant. I supposed I would find out soon enough.

The carriage turned in at the gate and started up the long elm-lined drive. An unexpected shiver chilled me as if a menacing shadow had fallen, darkening the sunlit October afternoon.

The closer we got to the house, the more tense I became. It was a sensation in direct contrast to the peaceful view from the carriage window — the smooth lawn sweeping down to the river, the leaves of the trees turning golden, the garden brilliant with tall flowers. It was difficult to imagine that fear or sorrow or anger or any violence could penetrate this pastoral, sheltered place.

And yet I knew better. Montclair had a history of its own. It had known the sound of laughter and of weeping and had been touched as often by tragedy as by joy.

I thought of Alair, the beautiful, capricious child who had grown up into a

charming, butterfly-woman and become
Mistress of Montclair before me. Did her
death still linger hauntingly?

I had no time to dwell on sorrowful possibilities, for the carriage had come to a
stop in front of the columned porch and
Ben was coming down the steps to assist
me with my luggage.

"Glad to see you back, miss — 'scuse
me, I mean, Missus." He grinned and
shook his head at his own slip.

"Where are the children, Ben?" I asked,
anxious to see them even after this short
separation.

"They's with Vinny. Think they plannin'
some kind of welcome-home celebration,"
he replied chuckling.

I hurried up the steps and into the house.
To my surprise, Randall was standing at
the open door to the library as I walked
into the hall.

He acknowledged my arrival with a brief
nod, then beckoned to me. "Come in here,
Druscilla. I want you to see the wedding
present that was delivered today."

I followed as he held the door wider for
me to pass through. Then, in a few quick
strides, he crossed the room to a large,
draped form and snatched away the covering cloth.

What I saw made me gasp.

"From my former in-laws, your aunt and uncle!" Randall announced, stepping aside.

There, in my startled view, was a full-sized portrait of Alair — not the vibrant woman she had been in life, but deathly pale, seated forlornly on an open coffin and holding a wilted white rose at her breast.

chapter
18

Within weeks of our return, it had become clear to me that the silver tray on the hall table reserved for calling cards left by the Mayfield gentry would remain empty, and the daily mail would bring no invitations. We were being snubbed by the entire county! Loyalty to Aunt Harmony and Uncle Clinton, I suspected, was behind it all.

At first I was deeply hurt, then I realized that Bondurant had never been received, even when he was married to my cousin. Perhaps that's why they had traveled so much, I mused. Such open rejection would have been humiliating to Alair.

I knew Randall was aware of it, too. Perhaps he had thought things would change once it was known he had married a Montrose, rightful heir to Montclair. But what cut him most was knowing he would never be invited to join the Hunt — the exclusive membership passed down from father to son, never open to an outsider, especially an outsider who had wrested an inheritance from one of their own.

I turned my attention to achieving the changes he wanted in the house. Gradually the rooms were redone, one by one, regaining their original lovely simplicity. The ornate furniture was carted away and the beautiful old pieces, restored and polished, took their places.

We never mentioned the bizarre portrait of Alair her parents had commissioned, then sent. Where it was stored or what Randall did with it, I never knew. I only remember the look on his face, where anger and pain conflicted.

One morning, when I came down to breakfast, I met Randall just coming in from his solitary early morning ride. He halted on his way to his own suite of rooms to change from his riding clothes and looked at me speculatively.

"Do you ride?" he asked brusquely.

"Not well," I admitted. "As children, we all used to scramble on the back of an old mare put out to pasture while she ambled about and grazed. Then, when I lived at Cameron Hall, Uncle Rod instructed me in the use of a lady's saddle. But when we moved to Richmond, we couldn't afford to keep a saddle horse —"

"Well, then, you must learn, and at once," Randall said firmly. "I'm getting ponies for the girls, and you can take lessons along with them. I'll speak to my head groom. He'll find a nice, gentle horse for you. One hour a day to begin with, then two and so on." He spoke with customary decisiveness. "Perhaps by next fall, you'll be ready to hunt. I mean to have my own hunting parties, invite friends. We don't need the Mayfield Hunt Club!" His contempt was visible in the way he slapped his crop against his thigh and marched down the hall to his rooms.

I wasn't at all sure I liked the idea. Of course, Uncle Rod had belonged to the Club. In fact, the Hunt always started from Cameron Hall. But the riders were all experts, a bit wild and reckless, I thought, leaping and cantering and thundering by, jumping impossible fences and tearing along the countryside.

But if it were so important to Randall —

Only a few afternoons later, Vinny brought two huge boxes to my bedroom. When I opened the first one, I found a handsome new riding habit — long fitted jacket and skirt of fine broadcloth in forest green, and a velvet bowler. Another box contained a pair of smooth leather boots. I slipped on the jacket. It fit perfectly. Then I tried on the hat, smoothing back my hair under the attached netting. Viewing myself in the full-length pier mirror, I felt a surge of satisfaction.

No wonder so many ladies rode, if one could look so elegant while doing so!

Lally and Nora were wildly excited over the ponies — a chestnut and a cinnamon-colored one — which Jed, the groom, led around to the front of the house on the first morning of riding instructions. Following him was a stable boy, leading a beautiful gray mare, saddled and ready to mount.

"This is 'Missy,' ma'am," Jed introduced me. "She's a sweet, easy-goin' lady," he told me after he had lifted the little girls into their saddles. "She'll make a fine horse for you, Miz Bondurant. Nothin' for you to worry 'bout."

With both children already seated on their mounts and observing me curiously, there was no escape. Reminding myself that all the Montrose women had been splendid riders and that I had to keep up the tradition, I lifted my skirt, stepped onto the mounting block, threw my right leg over the pommel, and found myself in the saddle. It felt very high off the ground.

Jed patted Missy's neck and said soothingly, "Now, jest settle back and relax. We're gonna walk down to the corral, slow and easy."

Soon, much of what Uncle Rod had tried to teach me came back — the proper way to hold the reins, to let the horse know what you expected, the proper posture. I began to enjoy the daily lessons and, little by little, gained confidence.

The girls were natural-born horsewomen, and soon Jed had them jumping low fences.

One morning, when I came into the dining room dressed in my riding habit, Randall was standing by the fireplace, sipping a cup of coffee. His eyes moved over me approvingly.

"So, how is it going?" he asked. "Jed tells me you're learning fast. You'll be ready to ride to the hunt next."

I shook my head doubtfully, but Randall did not seem to notice. He put his coffee cup on the mantel. "I'll be away for a few days — business." And giving me a brief nod, he left the room.

A few minutes later, I heard the carriage roll down the drive and was surprised by the feeling of abandonment I felt. My relationship with Randall, marriage certificate or no, had changed very little since my days as governess.

I shrugged away the onset of self-pity. I had entered into this arrangement, accepting its terms, and there was no use feeling sorry for myself now or longing for a companionship that was not forthcoming.

I drank my coffee. Then, picking up my gloves and riding crop, I went out the front door. It was a sparkling fall morning — the distant hills misted with blue, the air crisp and energizing on the walk down to the stables.

Missy was already saddled, waiting for me at the mounting block in front of the stables. I had been riding out by myself for a few weeks along the well-marked bridle paths at the edge of the meadows and in the woods around the river.

"Mawnin', missus." Jed tipped his beaked cap as he led out the children's ponies. "Sweet mawnin' for a ride," he called as I started out.

As Missy eased into her gentle rocking gait, I realized how much I had come to enjoy these peaceful rides. It was about the only time I had to explore the land around Bon Chance that had once been so familiar.

I rode deeper into the woods, crossing the curved rustic bridge over the wide creek that cut through the meadow, and passing the small, slant-roofed chapel that one of my ancestresses Avril Dumont Montrose had built to accommodate the many circuit-rider preachers who visited Montclair in the olden days. It was boarded up now, as were the windows of the little "honeymoon house" — Eden Cottage — set in a clearing nearby. Originally constructed as a model for the mansion, this was the place where Montrose men traditionally brought their brides for the first year of marriage.

There was so much of my family's history in these acres. I thought of all the lives that had been lived in the house, the generations of people who had loved, married, reared their children here, ridden through these same sun-dappled woods.

I leaned forward into the even canter of my horse, savoring the fresh autumn wind on my face, hearing its whispering in my ears. Far from responsibility or the thoughts that sometimes troubled me, I felt a new freedom, a peace different from anything I'd experienced.

Suddenly I was startled to hear the sound of a horse's hooves pounding over the pine-needled trail. It came upon me so unexpectedly I didn't have time to slow Missy to a walk or draw her to one side. Suddenly, looming before me in my direct path was a huge stallion, its rider bent over the saddle, approaching at full gallop.

I pulled hard on the reins — too hard for a horse unused to such a harsh tug on her sensitive mouth. She reared in protest, shaking her head and almost yanking the reins from my hand. Frightened, I clutched the edge of my saddle and stared, wide-eyed, at the oncoming horse and rider.

He was struggling with his own steed, cursing and issuing sharp commands. By the time he had quieted the prancing black horse, the docile Missy had come to a standstill, and I'd had a chance to get a good look at him.

Brett Tolliver!

The terrible day of his quarrel with Randall came back to me, in all its horror. My hands trembled on the reins.

When he straightened in the saddle, we were face to face. His eyes swept me brazenly. If the man were not completely drunk, there was no doubt that he had been drinking, for his complexion was mottled, his eyelids puffy, his mouth hard.

"What are you doing out here?" he demanded. "Nobody's ridden in these woods for years!"

My throat felt thick as I stammered, "Th— this is our property."

"*Your* property? Who are *you?*"

"Druscilla Montrose . . . Bondurant."

"*Bondurant?*" He spat out the name.

Missy moved restlessly, nervous with the big stallion so close. I lifted my reins and started to turn her in the path, but Brett moved faster. Edging his horse over to me, he grabbed my reins and thrust his face so close I could smell the strong odor of liquor on his breath.

Between clenched teeth, he said, "So that wretch Bondurant is back . . . and with another bride? Watch out! He's a Bluebeard, you know!"

I could see the red-veined whites of his protruding eyes. My breath caught in my throat. I leaned away from him, pulling at my reins to free them.

"He's living on borrowed time! Tell him that for me!" Brett snarled, then he loosened his grip on my reins so suddenly that I nearly lost my balance.

Then he gave Missy a sharp crack with his crop on her flanks. She whinnied and started with a jolt that almost unseated me. Whirling around, she began a jerky trot as

228

I slumped over her neck, grasping a handful of mane.

Finally I regained control of Missy, but tears rolled unchecked down my face I was so unnerved by the encounter with Tolliver. If he had not known we were back until today, I was terrified of what he might do — frighten the children when Randall or I were away? Return to further harass us? I had heard Randall promise to kill him if he ever stepped foot on our property again, but evidently he rode freely in the woods surrounding Bon Chance.

I shuddered, imagining what might transpire if these two men clashed again.

We were nearing the little chapel and, spontaneously, I drew Missy to a halt, then slipped out of my saddle and tethered her loosely to nibble on some grass while I walked up to the small steepled structure.

It was quiet in the woods now, with only the sound of my boots crunching the twigs and underbrush as I wandered around, trying to peer inside through the cracks of the boards. I remembered the small way-side shrines of Italy, the little rustic chapels built into the hillsides on the Swiss mountain paths. Something within me craved the sanctuary of just such a place of prayer.

I tried the door, but it was locked; I pried at the boarded windows but they would not budge. Fighting disappointment, I remembered that God is everywhere. One needed neither church nor cathedral to pray. He is as near as breath.

Impulsively, I knelt on the ground carpeted with pungent pine needles, and in the shadow of the wooden cross over the doorway. I put my head upon clasped hands and prayed for protection — for Randall, for the little girls, for myself.

I did not take that path through the woods again. For the rest of the week, I stayed well within sight of the corral, where the girls were practicing jumps, or out near the acres of pasture land. At the end of my hour, I rode back to the barn.

One day when I dismounted, allowing one of the stable hands to take Missy for her rubdown and bucket of oats, I saw Jed bringing the ponies back.

"Jed, there's a beautiful chestnut mare in the pasture I've never seen. Doesn't anyone ride her?"

A startled expression came over Jed's mahogany face, and he averted his eyes, fiddling with one of the ponies' bridles. "No ma'am. Don't nobody ride her. Not anymo'."

Puzzled, I waited for his explanation.

His head down, Jed mumbled, "She Miss Alair's horse . . . de one she was ridin' de day she got killed. Saucy — dat's her name. It wuz when she come back empty-saddled dat we knowed sumpin' was wrong."

Still not glancing up, Jed went on. "De day afta Miss Alair die, Mr. Randall come down here wid a shotgun, ready to shoot Saucy. Reckon he couldn't bring hissef to do it." Jed shook his head. "Mr. Randall jest put his head down on de fencepost and cry lak a baby. He tole us to put Saucy out to pasture."

My heart wrenched in sympathy. Randall was not the cold, unfeeling man he often appeared to be. I knew that, having observed him with his daughters. But hearing first-hand of his anguish over Alair's death confirmed it once again.

I tried to push the ugly encounter with Brett to the back of my mind. I certainly never intended to deliver his hateful message to Randall. The sooner I could forget him and the incident in the woods, the better.

Then one day, coming back into the house from a ride with the girls, I saw an envelope lying in the silver tray on the hall table.

Curious, I went over, picked it up, and saw it was addressed to me. I tore open the envelope and unfolded a sheet of thin, cheap paper.

As I read the words printed there, I drew in my breath in horror: HOW DOES IT FEEL TO BE MARRIED TO A MURDERER?

There was no signature. None was needed. I knew Brett Tolliver had written it.

Convulsively, my hand crumpled the paper into a ball. At that instant, I heard a noise behind me. Whirling around, I saw Randall standing at the front door.

chapter
19

Randall's unexpected return that day was
precipitated by an invitation to join in the
next morning's hunt at a plantation now
owned by some Northerners who were
friends of the Elliotts. Peggy and her mother
were guests there and had invited Randall to
come.

"Of course, as my wife you are included
in the invitation for the Hunt Breakfast,
the dinner and dance that evening."

"Oh, Randall, I think not —" I protested, dismayed at the idea of having to
make conversation with a group of people I
did not know while others hunted. Most of
all, the prospect of being in the company
of the Elliotts, mother and daughter, was
not very appealing.

Randall frowned, then shrugged aside
his momentary displeasure. "As you like,"
he said curtly. "Where are the girls?"

"They're still down at the corral with
Jed."

"Good. I want to see how they're progressing." And he turned and went out the door, setting out for the corral.

I stood there, watching him go, feeling the crumpled paper in my hand. Should I have shown it to Randall, confided in him about my encounter with Brett Tolliver in the woods? Uncertain, I finally decided to tear it up. Its bitter message had no place in the life we were trying to build here for these children who had already known such tragedy. It was the fevered distortion of a sick mind, shaping events to his own resentful imagining.

But even if I destroyed the note, could I prevent the possibility of Tolliver's carrying out his threats? Was it possible that the poison of his hatred could still destroy the fragile security and peace of this family?

I tried to put it all out of my mind as completely as I tore the paper into tiny shreds. But my sleep that night was fragmented. Brett's snarling face floated in and out of troubled dreams.

I woke at first light and went down for coffee to clear my light-headedness.

As I stood at the dining room window, sipping my coffee, looking out at the mist-clad morning, I heard the sound of boots on the polished floor of the hallway. Turning, I saw Randall enter the room.

He was dressed for the hunt in traditional attire — red fitted jacket, dove-colored breeches, shiny black boots, white stock and black velvet cap. It suited him perfectly, and I could not restrain a rush of pride that I was married to this man.

"I was going to leave word for you," he began after a brief nod. "I'll return after the hunt and breakfast. I've decided I want you to accompany me to the dinner party and dance tonight." He went over to the buffet, poured himself a cup of coffee, and drank it in a few gulps. "Wear one of your Paris gowns," he ordered on his way out.

Much as I dreaded it, I knew I had no alternative but to obey. I faced the evening ahead much as I imagined the French ladies of noble birth looked forward to the guillotine. If that were an exaggeration, it seemed a small one.

It would be my first venture into society as Randall's wife.

Oakhaven used to belong to an old Mayfield family, the Miltons. Like so many, they had lost it after the War. I had heard the wealthy Northerners who now owned the estate entertained on a grand scale.

Vinny, obviously delighted to use her

skills as a lady's maid, fussed and fretted as she helped me dress and do my hair.

"Nobody in Mayfield eber seen sumpin' lak dis, Miss Dru!" she exclaimed as she slipped my gown over my head and began buttoning the tiny buttons.

The little girls had been allowed to come in and perch on my bed to watch me get ready.

"Oh, Drucie, you're beautiful!" declared Nora.

"Beau-ti-ful!" echoed Lally, her rosy mouth forming an O.

The dress was stunning — a shimmering taffeta of violet-blue with a low-cut squared bodice, full puffed sleeves adorned with velvet violets, and a shirred net lavender overskirt.

Surveying myself critically in the full-length mirror, I knew the magnificent gown would flatter any woman who wore it. But some of my pleasure in looking my best was dimmed by the knowledge that the only reason Randall wanted me to accompany him tonight was to show me off. My Paris gown would be the envy of every woman there.

I recalled the stinging comment of a gruff old Englishman aboard ship who was deaf and did not realize how loudly his voice carried. One day, when I had been promenading on deck with Randall — a brisk, windy day that prompted me to wear my sable jacket — I had overheard Colonel Markham say, "American women are the peg their husbands hang their fortunes on. *She* is a walking advertisement of his wealth."

I had just finished my hair and put in my sapphire and pearl earrings when there was a knock at the bedroom door. Randall entered, carrying a slim, red leather jewelry box.

"This is for you to wear tonight," he said.

The little girls scrambled down from the bed to cluster close to me while I opened it. We all breathed a long sigh when we saw the lustrous pearls gleaming against the blue velvet.

It was a choker, the kind the lovely Princess Alexandra, bride of the Prince of Wales had made so popular in England — strands of matched pearls clasped by an oval sapphire.

"It's exquisite, Randall. Thank you," I murmured, lifting it out carefully. "It will be perfect with my earrings."

"I thought so."

I stared at him in pleased surprise. I didn't think he had ever noticed them.

"Some women are made to wear diamonds, some to wear pearls," was his reply.

Perhaps Randall had meant it as a compliment, I thought, as I fastened the choker. Yet I could not help wondering if he were comparing me to Alair's diamond-like beauty — rare, sparkling, precious.

Randall was silent on the drive over to Oakhaven, and his silence did nothing to ease my rapidly mounting apprehension about the evening ahead.

Our hostess, a Bostonian by her accent, greeted me cordially enough, her eyes taking in my gown, my jewelry, my ermine-trimmed velvet cape. To Randall, however, she was effusive in her welcome.

I took his arm as we entered the drawing room. Scanning the crowd, I picked out two familiar faces — that of Peggy Elliott and her mother.

It was a glittering evening. Fortunately, I had enough social poise, ingrained and instilled over the years, to carry off a confidence and ease I did not feel. I smiled, spoke, made light conversation even as I moved like someone in a pantomime. I might even have deemed my performance a success if it had not been for inadvertently becoming an eavesdropper.

After dinner, while the men lingered over conversation and cigars in the dining room and the women gathered in the drawing room, I went up to one of the bedrooms designated as the ladies' cloak and refreshing room.

Peggy Elliott's shrill nasal tones reached me before I entered and I stopped, unwilling to feign politeness to someone who had always tried to make me feel insignificant and inferior.

"I think young Mrs. Bondurant is very handsome, elegant —" someone said.

"Oh, yes, I suppose." I recognized Peggy's voice. "Her gown is superb, but she was as poor as a church mouse before she married Randall, you know. She was his children's *governess!*"

Now came Mrs. Elliott's pompous pronouncement. "I should have warned him. He was all alone, poor man, and with those pathetic little girls . . . well, it's obvious how she wormed her way into his life with her so-sweet Southern ways." The latter, spoken with heavy sarcasm.

"But wasn't she from one of the first families? A Montrose?" another asked.

"I'm so sick of hearing about the Montroses of Mayfield!" Peggy sneered. "Before the War they may have had all that land, slaves — what's that to be proud of? Who cares now?"

Afraid I'd lose control if I entered the room where I'd been the subject of such malicious gossip, I turned and hurried back downstairs.

Just as I reached the bottom step, the gentlemen were coming out of the dining room. I felt Randall's quick glance. He must have somehow perceived I was upset, for he moved quickly toward me.

"I think we could safely say our good nights and leave. If you are ready?"

I had never felt more grateful. Randall sent the maid up for my wrap and within minutes we had thanked our hostess and were in the luxurious seclusion of our carriage, heading home.

"Did you enjoy the evening?" he asked me.

"Well —" I began, wondering how I could tactfully tell the truth.

"Don't bother to be polite. After European society, I find this kind of evening provincial. But, one cannot live in isolation, and I must make a place for my daughters in Virginia society."

The last statement was uttered with a kind of intensity that bothered me. There was more to life than being accepted by a dubious stratum of society.

But then, I had never known that kind of rejection. As a Montrose, there had never been any question of my acceptance.

We reached Bon Chance just as the grandfather clock struck eleven. At the foot of the stairs, Randall bade me good night, adding, "Thank you for coming with me tonight. You were the handsomest woman there. I was very proud."

A thrill of hope fluttered within me. I felt warmed by his words. I searched his face, longing to see some glimpse of real caring in the dark eyes. But the moment ended. Randall bowed slightly, turned and went down the hall to his own suite of rooms. Slowly I mounted the steps, feeling suddenly weary.

Vinny had turned down my bed, laid out my nightgown and robe. The ruby-globed lamp was lighted, casting a rosy glow, and a cheerful fire was burning in the fireplace.

I put aside my wrap and walked toward my dressing table, taking out my hairpins as I did, letting my hair tumble to my shoulders.

The evening had been a strain and I was glad it was over. I was gratified that Randall had been proud of me tonight, but somehow it seemed an empty reward compared to the real desire of my heart.

I lifted my hands to unclasp the beautiful pearls and, as I did, my gaze fell on a square envelope propped against the mirror.

With shaking hands, I picked it up. I recognized the handwriting. My first reaction was to rip it apart without reading it. But curiosity won out.

THE WAGES OF SIN IS DEATH. MURDER IS SIN. DEATH IS THE PUNISHMENT FOR MURDERERS. YOUR COUSIN WAS MURDERED. YOU ARE LIVING WITH HER MURDERER.

I dropped the note as if it had burned my fingers.

If Brett Tolliver were writing these horrible letters, then how had he managed to get inside the house and into my bedroom?

chapter
20

Winter was slow in coming, and the lovely Indian summer lingered long into November. Peace seemed to settle in the valley like the blue haze over the hills. Yet, for me, there was no real peace. The insidious anonymous notes kept showing up at unforeseen times in unlikely places.

MURDER WILL OUT. HE MUST PAY.

DEATH OPENS UNKNOWN DOORS. HIS SECRET WILL BE DISCLOSED.

DAY OF RETRIBUTION NEAR. BE SURE, HIS SIN WILL FIND HIM OUT.

I'm not sure why I began to keep these vicious notes, not tear them up as I had the first one. Maybe I thought that by comparing them I could make some pattern of them, find out who was sending them. I was almost sure it was Brett Tolliver. I could understand his vengeful anger. But what if it were someone else? What if someone else out there suspected Randall of somehow being responsible for Alair's death?

The thought sent icy fingers of fear tracing along my spine.

The little pile of envelopes in my dressing table drawer grew week by week. Would the writer soon make his move? Come out from behind the veil of anonymity? If there were a shred of truth to his accusations, should I pursue it?

I shuddered with distaste. The cloud of mystery still hung over Alair's death, since the details had never been fully disclosed. Uncle Clint had said Randall was too distraught to speak coherently about it. But who was the doctor who had attended her? And would he know what had caused her death? Being thrown from a horse — as good a rider as Alair had been — did not seem entirely plausible.

Randall had never spoken to me of his marriage to Alair. Her name was never mentioned between us. But if anyone had evidence that Randall was responsible — as the writer of these dreadful notes implied and as Brett Tolliver certainly believed — why had he not come forward?

All these confusing, disquieting thoughts churned within me one day and I decided to seek out Vinny's old grandmother. Perhaps she could remember something that might give me a clue as to what had really happened. She was still supervising the kitchen when Alair married Randall, and I knew that everything that took place in a household eventually got back to the kitchen. If there had been foul play, she would surely have gotten wind of it.

I found the old woman sitting in the afternoon sunshine outside her little cabin.

"Afternoon, Tuley!" I greeted her as I approached.

She squinted into the sun as though trying to figure out who I was.

"It's Druscilla, Tuley, Miss Dove's little girl."

"Oh, shure, honey. Come on up." Her wrinkled black face broke into a toothless smile.

I tucked my skirt about me and sat on the wooden steps of the porch, near her woven-rush rocker.

"You wuz such a chubby lil' gel, and now you is all growed up into a pretty lady." She appeared to doze off. Then, just as I was about to prompt her, she spoke again. "Yes'm, time do go by. Seems lak yestiddy when all you chillun were itty-bitty, no bigger den toadstools."

Tuley had her own way of putting things. I remembered how she had described Alair the first time I visited her shortly after coming to Bon Chance as the girls' governess.

"Miss Alair wuz lak a hummin'-bird, a flittin' and flyin' to all de bright flowers . . . not stayin' long at any one, but takin' off afta a few sips of nectah."

In a way, it was a perfect description. Tuley was wise in a way that had nothing to do with education. So I wasted no time in launching into the reason for my visit, before she could doze off again.

"Was Miss Alair happy when she came here as mistress, Tuley? Were she and Mr. Bondurant happy together?"

Tuley compressed her lips and closed her eyes as if in deep thought. "Nobody but de Lawd knows fo' shure 'bout dat," she said slowly. "She shure had everythin' to make her happy." She shook her head. "She seem happy 'nuf. De babies made her happy . . . but den —"

Tuley was momentarily distracted when her old yellow tiger-striped cat who had been sleeping in the sun woke up, stretched, and leaped into her lap.

"Then what?" I prodded her memory.

"Cain't say fo' shure. Dey wuz gone fo' a long while, den when dey come back — Miss Alair she seem diff'rent." Again Tuley shook her head. "Mr. Brett took to comin' 'round."

"Brett Tolliver?"

"Yes'm. Dat's him." Her gnarled fingers stroked the cat, her eyes misted with tears. "An' den Miss Alair — den dere was de accident —"

I did not feel it was right to distress the old woman any more. She had confirmed my suspicion that Brett was behind, not only Alair's unhappiness, but was likely the sender of the anonymous letters.

So I changed the subject, complimenting Tuley on her sunflowers that were still blooming this late in the year. I left her some pears from the orchard I'd brought, then I said good-by and walked back to the house, deep in thought.

What should I do now? Should I go see Brett, demand to know what he knew about Alair's death? The thought terrified me. If his allegations somehow implicated Randall, I really didn't want to know.

That afternoon I forced myself to admit my real feelings for Randall. That, in spite of everything, I loved him and longed for him to love me. Between us now, however, was the unresolved mystery of Alair's death.

Nearing the house, I stood for a moment leaning against one of the giant elms, putting my tumultuous thoughts into some kind of order. As I did, the Scripture verse came clearly into my mind: "Ye shall know the truth, and the truth shall set you free."

If I sought the truth and found out that the accusations in the letters were lies, then I could rid myself of the dark shadow of suspicion hovering over Randall.

But what if I found out they were true?

I shuddered, but even then I knew I had no alternative.

As if in confirmation of what I knew I must do, another letter arrived, slipped under the door at the very moment I was visiting Tuley.

IF YOU WANT TO KNOW THE TRUTH ABOUT ALAIR'S DEATH MEET ME. DATE, TIME, PLACE IN NEXT LETTER.

chapter
21

As if its fury had been stored up by its long delay, winter arrived with a vengeance. The first week in December snow blanketed the ground. The children were ecstatic, and we spent many happy hours building snowmen and sliding down the slopes on makeshift sleds. Virginia snow, unlike that in New England, never lasted long, but the cold weather did.

Ironically, when the snow came, the anonymous letters stopped. The horrible strain of never knowing when to expect that letter suggesting a time and place to meet to learn the identity of the writer, finally wore away. I was limp with relief. Maybe whoever was playing this cruel game had given up.

Just then, some happy news displaced my anxiety. Jonathan would be spending the Christmas holidays at Cameron Hall since Aunt Garnet, who had brought him up, and her husband, Jeremy Devlin, would be visiting Auntie Kate.

I was thrilled at the prospect of seeing Jonathan. It had been over two years since we had been together, although we had kept in touch by letter.

It was the Camerons' tradition to hold Open House on Christmas Day, and I particularly looked forward to this festive gathering.

We were sitting at the breakfast table when our invitation arrived, and after reading it, Randall tossed it toward me. "This is the first time in the nearly twelve years I've lived in Mayfield that I've been invited. That must say something for being married to a Montrose."

I started to protest, then thought better of it. "You do want to go, don't you?" I asked. "You haven't met Jonathan, and I know Auntie Kate would love to see the girls."

Randall went on opening his own mail. At last, he replied, "If it will please you to see your relatives, of course we'll go."

That indifferent compliance had to satisfy me, but I was determined to make our first Christmas as a family a special occasion. When I broached the subject of attending the Midnight Service at Mayfield's community church, I was not sure Randall would agree.

I did not know him well enough to know if it was mockery I saw in his eyes when he said, "By all means! Let us keep all the Montrose traditions!"

I might have suspected sarcasm if I had not observed that he often masked his real emotions with such a remark.

As it happened, it was Randall himself who, on Christmas Eve afternoon, suggested the girls take a nap so they would not be sleepy when we left for the service.

Happily, a light snowfall covered the ground the day before, and Randall had the sleigh readied for our trip to church. Bundled in furs and blankets, we set off over snowy fields under a frosted moon. Church bells were ringing with a sweet clarity in the night air as we entered the small stone building.

Inside, candlelight glowed softly while the organ played the gentle ancient hymns. The little girls were quiet, taking in everything with an innocent reverence.

Afterwards, when we left the church, the air was so clear and sharp that it almost hurt to breathe. We skimmed home over the iced rutted road to hot mulled cider and cake laid out for us, and presents to open.

Nora and Lally, as usual, had dozens of gifts Randall had ordered for them both from a famous toy store in New York, as well as from abroad. The one that turned out to be their favorite was an enormous hand-carved Noah's Ark, complete with pairs of all the animals. They had spotted it in a store in Germany and had been fascinated by it.

"Here's another for you, Drucie," Nora said, handing me an oblong package, wrapped in a lovely piece of silk and tied with a lace ribbon.

When I opened it I found inside a beautiful porcelain shepherdess figurine. I looked up in surprise to see Randall watching me.

I lifted it out of the excelsior in which it nestled. It was so delicate and lovely.

"Oh, Randall, thank you! How did you guess?" I asked breathlessly. I had admired it in a shop in Austria, touching it carefully with my fingers, hardly daring to pick it up. Evidently he had arranged to buy it at some later time as a Christmas surprise.

"I thought you would like it," he said casually, then began to thank Lally for the pen-wipers she had so laboriously sewn for him with her stubby little fingers.

I made a pretense at examining the fragile figurine, too overcome with emotion to look at Randall again. I was afraid he would read in my eyes the love I felt for him. That he had gone to that much trouble for me must mean he cared. *It had to,* I thought with a quickened heartbeat.

We all went to bed soon after and, in my room, I placed the little shepherdess on my dressing table where I could see it every day. I could not get over the fact that Randall had selected something with such care to give me.

The sun, glancing off the untrampled whiteness covering lawns, meadows, and fields, stung our eyes as we drove over to the party at Cameron Hall on Christmas afternoon.

I was hardly out of the sleigh when Jonathan came bounding down the steps, picked me up, and swung me around. "It's so good to see you, Dru! Let me look at you! Here you are a married lady. I can tell you cousin Norvie was heartbroken when he heard you'd got yourself married over in Italy last summer. He was all set to ask you to come to the Fall Germans with him!" Jonathan teased.

I laughed gaily, thinking that attending a set of college dances at Harvard was the farthest thing from my mind last summer. Handsome as he was, Norvell Meredith seemed a mere boy compared to Randall.

Suddenly I remembered I had not introduced my husband to my cousin. I turned to see the little girls staring and smiling, but Randall did not seem amused.

"Randall, this is my cousin Jonathan. You remember . . . I've told you how the two of us . . . and Alair . . . grew up together."

Though Randall bowed politely, I felt the icy reserve before he turned away, while Jonathan and I, chatting simultaneously, tried to bring each other up to date on all that had transpired since we had last been together.

So intrigued was I with Jonathan's account of life at Harvard that I failed to notice the subtle rebuff of my relatives' friends. Auntie Kate could not have been more gracious and Uncle Rod was a correct, courteous host, but I realized at length that their guests were not ready to extend a warm welcome to us. There was no overt rudeness, of course, but as we moved from the dining room, where the sumptuous buffet was set up, small groups of people simply closed their ranks, deliberately excluding us. Others merely avoided my glance, pretending not to see me.

I looked around for my family, but the

little girls were playing with other children in the parlor especially set aside for them. Then I saw Randall standing alone. He appeared nonchalant, sipping a glass of punch. But I saw the set of his jaw, the line of his mouth.

I was angry and hurt. Randall was as much a gentleman as any man here. I knew if it were not for me, he would have stalked out. He had agreed to come for my sake. Now I must rescue him.

I touched Jonathan's sleeve. "Jonathan, dear, I must go."

He looked surprised, disappointed. "Go? But you've only just come. We have so much to talk about that you can't leave now."

"I must." I lowered my voice. "Randall is not comfortable. He doesn't know anyone and no one is making any effort to speak to him. Of course, it's because of Aunt Harmony and Uncle Clint . . . but I can't go into it all now. You must come over and spend some time with me at Montclair — Bon-Chance."

"I'd like that. I haven't seen the place since I left, you know," Jonathan said eagerly.

"We've been restoring it. Randall wanted it all put back the way it used to be. You'll love seeing it. It looks the way your mother would have remembered it."

"Great! I shall be here all next week. But, before you go, Dru, I must tell you my most important news. I have given Davida an engagement ring! We're to be married in June, right after my graduation from Harvard."

"Oh, Jonathan! How marvelous!" I hugged him. "You must tell me all about it when you come. Now, I better collect the children and say good-by to Auntie Kate."

Randall stared straight ahead as he drove us home through the purple dusk of the early winter afternoon. The children's happy chatter covered his silence.

Back at Bon-Chance, I took two weary little girls upstairs, helped them undress. Lally was almost asleep on her feet. They were both worn out from being up so late on Christmas Eve and the long day filled with fun and excitement. After I'd tucked them in, I went back downstairs.

I found Randall in the library. One arm was propped on the mantelpiece, and he was staring morosely into the fire.

"May I come in?" I asked. I wanted to say something to minimize the sting of his ostracism at the party, but I didn't know what to say.

"Yes, do."

"I just wanted to ask if it would be all right with you if I had my cousin Jonathan over to stay a few days."

He gave a harsh laugh. "Of course! Let us be shining examples of Southern hospitality — not the sort we saw so prominently displayed this afternoon." He bit off the sharp words.

"Oh, Randall, I'm sorry —"

"Don't be! I'm used to Mayfield's brand. Besides, it doesn't mater. Invite *all* your relatives, why don't you? I won't be here anyway. I'm leaving — tomorrow probably — I'm going to New York, then on to Boston. Business mainly. Although I may see friends. People who enjoy my company. Southerners don't have a corner on gracious entertaining."

I twisted my hands helplessly. I felt so bad for him but I could offer no comfort. He would have rejected any attempt on my part to explain or excuse.

"Thank you, Randall." I turned to leave, then added, "Have a good trip."

It seemed a melancholy ending to a day otherwise filled with such happiness. The pang of loneliness I felt in anticipation of Randall's leaving was somewhat assuaged by my joy at the prospect of Jonathan's visit.

chapter
22

It was like old times when Jonathan came to
Bon Chance . . . Montclair! The children
adored him on sight, for Jonathan was still a
boy at heart in spite of his height and the
new mustache he had grown since I last saw
him.

He entered into all their games and in-
vented new ones. He got down on the floor
with them to play with the Noah's Ark and
after supper it was he who suggested a ri-
otous game of Blindman's Bluff or Hide 'n
Seek.

Growing up in the warm, family circle of
the Merediths, Jonathan had a natural ease
and a happy outlook on life. Having left to
live in the North when still a little boy, he
had not grown up surrounded by adults
who knew deprivation, defeat, and despair.
He had also inherited his mother's sweet
personality, along with her beautiful dark
eyes.

He stood for a long time in front of her

portrait which hung beside the other Brides of Montclair along the wall next to the staircase.

"I wish I'd known her —" he sighed — "or at least remembered her. All I have of her is what Uncle John has told me."

One evening after the children had gone to bed, Jonathan and I sat before the fireplace in my sitting room, reminiscing. We exchanged memories of the long-ago days when we had lived here with Aunt Garnet, Aunt Harmony, and Mama during the War.

"It's hard to believe there was a War going on," said Jonathan, shaking his head. "Mostly I remember you, Alair, and me having fun, playing. I do remember the day the Yankees came and took away my pony though! I remember how Aunt Garnet ran out and tried to stop them. Mighty brave of her. Good old 'Bugle Boy'." Jonathan smiled in retrospect.

We sat in companionable silence for a few minutes. Then Jonathan asked, "Have you ever seen the secret passage?"

"Secret passage?"

"Yes. The one Uncle John told me was used to hide slaves escaping North on the Underground Railroad."

"Underground Railroad?" I was beginning to sound like an echo. "Here? At Montclair?"

"Of course. Didn't you know about it? My mother was involved."

"Helping slaves escape? *Aunt Rose?*" I thought of the delicate beauty in the portrait who looked as though the most difficult task she would ever have was lifting a teacup. "You must be mistaken, Jonathan."

"No. It's true. Uncle John told me. Evidently my mother wrote him about it. Of course, the Montroses never knew about her activities."

"You mean she hid slaves right here under Uncle Malcolm's nose? And Grandfather's and Grandmother's?"

"I'm telling you it's the truth, Dru. I've read the letters my mother wrote to Uncle John."

It took me a full minute to absorb this astounding information.

Then Jonathan got to his feet. "Let's see if we can find it. It's in the old nursery above the master bedroom." He grinned. "I guess I slept through all those historic events."

We left my rooms and went downstairs to the suite of rooms occupied by Randall. I felt a little strange going in while he was away, and wondered what Jonathan really thought of us having separate apartments.

Randall's bedroom seemed austere, with not a single feminine touch. We found the door that opened onto a narrow winding staircase.

"I never knew about this," I remarked as we started up.

"In one of her letters, my mother explained that having the nursery built like this gave the mother both privacy and easy access to the baby. That way, the baby's nurse could come and go from the hall without disturbing the parents."

"You know a whole lot more about this house than I do, Jonathan!" I declared.

At the top of the steps, Jonathan lifted the oil lamp higher and looked around. The room seemed full of shadows.

"Where should we look?" I asked.

"Mother said there was a concealed spring along the wall. If you touch it, it releases a section of wall that slides back." Jonathan set down the lamp, and we both began feeling the paneling with open palms. "Ah, here it is!" he exclaimed, and I heard a creaking noise as the wall shifted to one side.

Jonathan picked up the lamp again and we both peered into a small room.

"Imagine!" I breathed. "How long do

you think people were kept in here?"

"Not long," Jonathan replied. "I understand this only leads to the tunnel that goes underground to the river. There they were met by a boat that took them further upstream to the next station of the Underground Railroad."

We stepped inside, and I shuddered as the lamp cast grotesque shadows on the rough walls.

"Here's the door!" Jonathan cried, his voice tinged with excitement. "It's bolted but I can move it, I think."

I grabbed his sleeve. "No, Jonathan! Don't! No telling what's beyond —" I shivered with horror. "Rats! Bats! Who knows?"

Jonathan hesitated. "All right," he agreed, acquiescing to my wishes. "At least, we've seen this much. It's given me a good idea how courageous my mother really was."

We returned to the room and slid the wall panel shut again.

"I wonder how many other secrets this house has kept," Jonathan mused aloud as we went downstairs, then back to my small parlor where a fire crackled cheerily.

"We Montroses have quite a heritage, Dru," Jonathan commented thoughtfully when we were comfortably settled in the deep chairs opposite each other. "Our past is all part of our present, everything is connected and the twists and turns of chance and fate affect our destiny."

"In what way?"

"For example, if my father, Malcolm, had not been sent North to be educated at Harvard, he would never have been Uncle John's friend and through him met and fallen in love with my mother. She would probably have married Kendall Carpenter, who is Davida's father. So, it seems we've come full circle."

I thought of my sense of destiny in meeting Randall, becoming Alair's children's governess and then agreeing to marry their father.

As if reading my mind, Jonathan interrupted abruptly. "Are you happy, Dru? I spoke to Randall briefly at Christmas Day, so I don't know him, only a fleeting impression —" He broke off and, spearing me with those truth-seeking eyes, posed the question.

I answered it with another question. "Can someone who is himself unhappy make anyone else happy?"

"Are you speaking of Alair . . . or yourself?"

"Oh, Jonathan, I don't know!" I sighed. If there were anyone in the world I could trust, it would be my cousin, but I didn't want to burden him with my problems. Besides, there was absolutely nothing he could do about it in the short time he would be visiting.

Sensing my reluctance to pursue the subject, Jonathan closed our discussion. "Well, at least this house is back in the family now. Whatever they call it . . . it will always be Montclair to me."

I decided to travel as far as Richmond with Jonathan on his way back North. Mama hadn't been able to leave Aunt Nell to come to Mayfield for the holidays, so it would be an opportunity for a visit with her as well as to prolong my time with my beloved cousin.

Jonathan stayed overnight with us at Aunt Nell's and, before he left on the train to Boston, Mama made him promise to bring his bride south as soon as possible.

"I promise, Aunt Dove. I'm longing for you to meet her and for her to meet all my Southern relatives. I just wish that all of you could come to the wedding."

After Jonathan left, Mama and I settled down for a nice visit. She was quite overcome with all the gifts I had brought for our belated Christmas celebration.

"You've been wickedly extravagant, I'm afraid!" she exclaimed as she held up the quilted velvet wrapper trimmed with lace. But I knew from the expression on her face that she was delighted with all the presents, especially the sewing box that played a Viennese waltz when the lid was lifted.

We spent many cozy hours together but, try as I might, I could not avoid the inevitable question. "Is there anything wrong, dear? Something seems to be troubling you."

Since my mother is usually sensitive and perceptive, I knew it would be useless to try to conceal what was on my mind and heart.

"Well, Mama, to tell the truth —" I began, and I launched into the events of the past months since returning from Europe. I told her about the disturbing encounter with Brett Tolliver in the woods and the subsequent series of anonymous letters.

"Poor man!" Mama shook her head sadly. "I hear he has been quite ill. A heavy cold, nearly went into pneumonia. Of course, he doesn't take care of himself, living alone as he does above the stables at his family's old place. The new owners are gone most of the year. It seems one of the Tollivers' old servants who sharecrops on the land found him in a delirious state and brought the doctor."

That could explain the sudden cessation of the letters I thought. That is — if Brett truly were the author.

"It is sad to see a great family come to such a bitter end," Mama said, sighing. "It seems like yesterday when Melissa Tolliver used to bring Brett over to play with you children. The Tolliver place was on the other side of the woods from Montclair and just as isolated. She longed for the company of other women, for she was alone there while Tom was away during the War." Mama shook her head, smiling a little in recollection.

"Brett was a rascal, full of mischief. He and Alair were the same age, and what a pair they were together. I remember one day when Melissa was ready to go home, and we couldn't find either of them. They had simply disappeared! We looked everywhere, getting more frantic by the minute. Over an hour later we finally found them down by the river, miles from the house — neither one of them a bit repentant that they'd caused such worry!"

Suddenly the pieces of the puzzle fell into place. While they were still children, Alair and Brett must have discovered the secret passageway! Being the adventurous sort, they undoubtedly followed it all the way to the river that day the adults thought they were lost. It was their secret. Afterwards, maybe they used it as a meeting place. If so, this seemed a logical explanation as to how the anonymous letters got into the house so mysteriously.

The thought of his sneaking up through the tunnel, letting himself in by the hidden panel and into my bedroom made me ill. Obviously, Brett Tolliver was bent on revenge, sowing seeds of suspicion about the man he hated. Yet . . . there was still the remote possibility that Brett might be right —

"Mama, do you think there is anything to these accusations?"

She looked startled. "That Randall Bondurant is in some way responsible for Alair's death? Why, I don't see how he could be. But then, you know the man so much better than I, dear!"

"Do I?" I deliberately let the question hang between us for a long moment, turning a significant gaze upon my mother.

"Dru, dear, what on earth are you

saying? That you don't know your own husband?" Mama's incredulous voice held a gentle reproach.

"I don't know if you'd understand, Mama, but —" I paused — "Randall married me mainly to give his little girls a stepmother. He wanted to be sure they would be reared —" and here I smiled — "as true Southern ladies."

"I'm sure he really only meant that he wanted to be certain they would be brought up by someone who loved and cared for them as only real kin could," Mama amended. "But you *do* love him, don't you, dear?"

"Yes, I love him, Mama. It's just that . . . I don't know how he feels about me." My anxiety was betrayed by my shaky voice.

"Many marriages are begun for practical reasons but become idyllic unions in time," Mama said comfortingly.

"He's so — so secretive, so mysterious about his own family background."

"Well, I can tell you a little about that," she said confidently. "My friend, Jocelyn Milton, was originally from Charleston and when she heard my daughter had married a Bondurant, she wasted no time in telling me that the Bondurants were from a very old French Huguenot family who were among the earliest settlers."

"Then why is he so reluctant to discuss his past?"

"Jocelyn also told me something I thought you would have known by now . . . that when Randall was a high-spirited, reckless young man, he disgraced the family name . . . or at least his father thought he did . . . so he disowned him."

"That's all you know?"

"Obviously, it did not keep him from making a great success of his life as well as accumulating enormous wealth."

At this point in our conversation, we heard the tinkle of the silver bell at Aunt Nell's bedside. It was Mama's summons and we had to break off our talk.

I left the next morning by train for Mayfield.

When I reached Bon Chance, I found Randall waiting for me . . . and another anonymous letter.

chapter
23

I spotted the letter at once. Seeing my name scrawled in the familiar handwriting sickened me. At the same time I became aware of Randall standing in the open door of the library.

"You're back!" I exclaimed. "I didn't expect you so soon!"

I moved to the hall table. In the act of casually removing my kid gloves, I slipped the envelope into my muff.

"Yes, it is sooner than I expected as well." A smile tugged at his lips. "When you have seen the children and refreshed yourself from your trip, please join me. I'll have Ben bring tea in here. I have some things to discuss with you."

"Of course, Randall," I murmured almost absentmindedly. All my attention was centered on the unknown contents of the envelope whose sharp edges I could feel inside my muff.

The joyful cries of welcome from Nora

and Lally seemed strangely muted, drowned out by my clamoring heartbeat.

Why had this letter come today, spoiling my homecoming, poisoning the atmosphere with its venom?

The children followed me into my bedroom, telling me how much they had missed me, plying me with questions about Jonathan, asking when they could meet my mother in Richmond. They bounced on my bed, chattering so constantly I could not gather my thoughts.

They leaned on their elbows at my dressing table while I removed my bonnet and tidied my hair.

"Listen, my darlings," I said at last. "Your Papa wants to see me, so I must go downstairs at once. I'll be up later to hear all your stories." I hugged each one and kissed their rosy cheeks.

Still, they clung to my hands as I made my way down the hall to the top of the staircase, so I had no chance to open or read the letter.

We parted with more hugs and kisses and I went down the steps, my mind still in turmoil.

Ben had brought in the tea service and was just stoking the fire when I entered the library. The curtains had been drawn against the early winter evening and the firelight brightened the room. But it did nothing to dispel my sense of impending doom. The letter's evil message hovered ominously, chasing away any comfort or security to be derived from the cheerful atmosphere of the room.

I tried to push back my gloomy presentiments as I poured tea, handed Randall his cup, then added sugar and lemon to my own. I sipped it gratefully, hoping its warmth would soothe my nervous chill.

Sitting opposite me in the deep, wing chair, Randall seemed less tense than usual. The firelight and the candleglow from the sconces on the mantelpiece played across the rugged contours of his face. Perhaps it was only the light, but it seemed to me that his expression was less stern and forbidding. I noticed, too, that he looked thoughtful, his attitude even somewhat pensive.

The thought passed through my mind that he had called me in to announce another move, another change, and immediately I thought of the packing and planning that would be needed. In a way it would be a relief, a means of escaping the terrible shadow of the letters.

Then he broke the silence. "I've been

doing a great deal of thinking while I've been gone . . . about the children, about the future. I left here in pursuit of some diversion, some group of which I'd feel a part. Always before, the company of crowds has satisfied my restlessness, my boredom."

He paused, shrugged. "The antidote did not work this time. Why? Because the patient had misdiagnosed his ailment."

What kind of riddle was Randall presenting?

He glanced into the fire. "You see, Dru, I was seeking happiness in the wrong place. It only took me a few days to realize that my happiness is here."

I looked at him in surprise. This certainly was not what I'd anticipated.

"The last two years have been the happiest of my life, the most contented. When I realized this, I asked myself why. Do you know the answer, Dru?"

I shook my head, still puzzled by this strange conversation.

Randall smiled. "The answer surprised even *me*, I must confess."

My heart began to thump wildly, and I felt my face flush. I tried to still my fluttering pulse. Could this be happening?

Randall continued to regard me with a

curious mixture of intensity and calculation. "Can you guess the reason, Dru?" he pressed.

My hand began to shake and I set my cup down so it would not rattle in its saucer. I avoided his gaze, turning instead to the red-orange flames dancing in the fireplace. What was Randall trying to say? A bright spurt of hope sprang up within me.

"Perhaps your modesty constrains you from what you must surmise is the truth." Randall paused again. "It is *you*, Druscilla, who has made the difference. You have made this place a home — a place worth coming home to, a place I long for now when I'm away."

I could scarcely believe my ears. I dared not allow myself to think what he might mean by his words.

"Look at me, Druscilla," he commanded gently.

Obediently I lifted my head. He was gazing at me with the tenderness I had seen in his eyes when he looked at the children. My heart turned over.

"I have always found you to be a person of honesty, of unwavering integrity. I want an honest answer from you now. What are your true feelings for me?"

His eyes held mine, demanding my answer.

"I have a great deal of admiration and respect —" I began haltingly.

He made an impatient gesture. "Respect is what we owe. Love is what we give. I don't want your respect — I want your love."

I stared at him, stunned.

"Obviously, this comes as some surprise," he said, and he got up, began to pace, hands clasped behind his back. "I have even denied it to myself. Told myself I should not cross the lines we drew, the terms of our agreement, the marriage contract we signed. But I left no room for emotion. I gave no thought to how feelings can change, deepen."

He stopped pacing, spun around and faced me, frowning. "There is no need for you to answer me now. This comes, I realize, without warning. But the need to tell you how I feel compelled me. . . . Druscilla, you are everything I dreamed a mother of my children should be, but more than that . . . everything I ever dreamed in a wife."

I could still find no words. Overwhelming emotion tied my tongue and stung my eyes with tears.

"There is more," Randall went on. "I know now it was wrong to marry without love. Worse still, that I did it a *second* time. I know now I never really loved Alair. I wanted her, wanted to possess her because she was a symbol of everything I lacked and coveted. The most beautiful, elusive creature, from one of the oldest, most prestigious families in Virginia — she was some sort of prize to be won."

He appeared now to have forgotten I was present, seemed to need to confess all that had weighed him down for so long.

"I think I knew even then it was a mistake. I tried to make up for it by lavishing every material comfort upon her, to compensate her with every luxury, every extravagance for that which I couldn't give her — love. At least, we had our beautiful children . . . but even the children didn't make Alair truly happy."

Somehow I got to my feet. "Randall, I don't think you should say any more."

"But what I'm trying to say, Dru, is that you deserve so much more than I was willing to give you in Italy at the time we married. I'm ready to give it now — that is — if you will accept it."

He caught both my hands in his, forcing me to look at him. "I wonder now if I prevented you from finding a real love with that young Italian? If I had not asked you to marry me, using the girls and your love for them as my reason, would you have married Orsini?"

I shook my head. "No, Randall."

"You're sure?"

"Yes," I said, not admitting that *he* had been the real reason I could not.

Randall looked relieved. "Then, do you think it is possible our relationship can change, become more?" he asked.

How strange life is, I thought. Months, even weeks ago, I would have given anything to hear Randall declare his love for me. Now the very words I had longed to hear were mired by the mystery that surrounded Alair's death. How could I love without reservations a man that may have been responsible for her death? What other horrible revelations might the unopened letter upstairs reveal? These terrible thoughts clouded my mind, and I withdrew my hands from Randall's.

"I can't answer any of this now. I need time —"

"Of course, I understand that. If your answer is no, we shall go on as before," he said.

But could we? After what had been said

tonight, could things ever be the same?

I mounted the broad staircase in a daze. Mechanically, I moved past Vinny, who was on her way down, looking at me curiously as she went by.

Entering the bedroom, I sat down at my dressing table and glanced at my reflection. My eyes were glazed, my face pale in the subdued light of the boudoir lamps. Then my eyes fell on my muff and I reached out and withdrew the letter.

For one frozen minute I vacillated between tearing it up and tearing it open. Then, I knew I had to read it. If I were ever to be free of lingering doubt, free to accept Randall's love, I had to find out the truth — whatever it was.

But would my passion for the truth destroy us all?

chapter
24

A crudely drawn hourglass and the words written in a scraggly downhill scrawl — TIME IS RUNNING OUT — staggered across the top of the page.

At the bottom was the date of the proposed rendezvous — TOMORROW AT 3 P.M. — AT THE COW-SHELTER ON THE RIDGE WHERE THE TOLLIVER AND MONTROSE PROPERTY ADJOINS. Then, as if in an afterthought — IF YOU AREN'T AFRAID OF THE TRUTH.

I don't know how long I sat there, holding the paper, reading it over and over. I do know that time seemed to stand still.

A knock at the door startled me, and I shoved the note under my hand mirror. "Who is it?"

"Randall. May I speak to you for a minute?"

Surprised, I rose and hurried to open the door.

"Dru, I just wanted to say that I hope

what I said earlier hasn't upset you. Perhaps, I shouldn't have spoken as I did. But I believe there is great possibility of much happiness for us — for *all* of us — and I didn't want it to slip away without making an attempt to grasp it."

My heart was too full to speak. Randall was offering me what I'd dreamed of, yearned for, but I wasn't free to take it. Not yet. Not while Alair's death was still shrouded in mystery.

"I hope I haven't offended you. If what I'm asking isn't possible, nothing need change. Certainly, I would not want to disturb your relationship with the girls."

"Nothing could ever change that," I said firmly.

"Good night then," Randall said, yet without making a move to go. I felt his eyes upon me, searching, beseeching.

Afraid I might betray my real feelings for him, I began to close the door. "Good night, Randall."

"Sleep well," he called.

But there was no sleep for me. My fear of what I might learn tomorrow kept me wide awake for hours, staring into the darkness.

The hope that I would not hear the evidence the letters claimed struggled against the possibility of truth I could not deny.

Getting away the next afternoon proved to be a problem. The children dawdled over lessons, there was a squabble between Vinny and the downstairs maid that had to be settled, and worst of all, Randall stayed around the house most of the morning instead of riding out or going into Mayfield.

At lunch he sent word that he wanted to watch the girls' riding lesson in the afternoon.

Since I was the one who usually supervised their lesson, I wondered if Randall might think this an opportunity for us to be together.

I did not want to be alone with Randall until I'd seen Brett. So after Jed led out Missy and the ponies, I told the girls to begin without me, explaining that I needed some trotting practice on one of the trails bordering the pasture.

The day was overcast. Gray clouds hung low over the hills, adding to my feelings of unease. I gave Missy her head to cover as much distance as possible before turning up the hill to the meeting place Brett had designated.

It was windy at the top of the hill. What must have once been lush meadows for herds of grazing cattle were now barren and brown. The shelter mentioned in the note was a dilapidated rubble of rotted timber, the roof falling down.

Missy was restless. She shook her head, whinnying nervously. I planned to remain seated on my horse during the meeting. It would be easier to escape should Tolliver become violent again. My heart was pounding in my throat.

From here, I could see all the way down into the valley. In the distance was a big, rambling house. The Tollivers', I imagined, though I had never noticed it before.

A light rain began to fall. I let Missy walk around a little as I searched the surroundings for some sign of Brett. But there was no one in sight. I knew if it started raining harder, I would be expected back at Bon Chance.

I could delay no longer. Either I rode home without seeing Brett and hearing what he had to say, or I could ride down the hill to the Tolliver stables and look for him there.

It was a rash decision, but once made, I lost no more time. The ground was getting damp and slippery as I guided Missy down the steep slope.

I knew the mare was sensitive to my

every movement, the pressure of my knee against her side, my inner turmoil or tranquility. Missy's ears twitched as I tightened the reins when we reached the bottom of the hill, and I slowed her to a walk.

The Tolliver place was deserted. There didn't seem to be anyone around. Thunder rumbled overhead, and the sky was darkening rapidly. I went around the house and back toward the barn. Still, I saw no one.

Had Brett changed his mind? Forgotten our meeting? Maybe, he thought I wouldn't come.

Looking up, I saw a dim light in one of the windows of the barn's upper story. Mama had told me Brett lived above the stables. I rode closer.

"Mr. Tolliver! Brett Tolliver!" I called.

Around the side steps led to a door at the top. As I held Missy to a standstill, the door creaked open and a hulking figure, wrapped in a blanket, stood there. He motioned with his hand.

"Come up!" he called hoarsely.

This was my moment of decision. I could turn around now and get out of here as fast as Missy could run. But something else compelled me. I dismounted, looped my reins on the hitching post under the roof's overhang.

My knees were trembling as I climbed the stairs.

Brett stepped back inside, holding the door open wider for me to enter. The room was nearly bare. One low-burning oil lamp in the high-raftered room cast a meager light. There was a table, two straight chairs, an unmade bunk in one corner. An open bottle of whiskey and a tumbler half full were on the table.

"Wasn't sure you'd come. Plucky lady, aren't you?" Brett shuffled over and pulled out a chair for me. "I've been sick. Couldn't ride out on a day like this." Punctuating his remark was a rattling cough.

"Seat? No? Drink? No?" He laughed harshly. *"Medicinal,"* he said, pouring more into the glass and taking a long sip. "For *me!* Hah!"

I put both hands on the back of the chair to steady myself, hoping my inner trembling didn't show. "Now that I've proved I wasn't afraid to come, what can you tell me about my cousin's death?"

His burning eyes flashed. "Alair was in love with me, you know. She was going to run away with me. It was all set. She was coming to meet me like in the old days by the river and we were going off together." Brett took another swallow of whiskey.

"But Randall followed her. There was an argument. He wanted her to come back with him. She didn't want to go, but he was on horseback, too . . . tried to grab the reins of her horse, but she broke away . . . galloped her horse . . . him in hot pursuit. She looked back to see if he was gaining on her . . . didn't see the low-hanging branch of a tree . . . was knocked off her horse —" Brett's voice broke. "It was . . . horrible! She lay there so white, still, blood running down her face, matting her beautiful blond hair —"

Brett put his head down on his arms on the table, his shoulders shaking in great, gulping sobs.

I had never been exposed to such raw emotion, had never seen a man weep openly. But one cold detached part of my mind kept asking, *Is he telling the truth? Is that what really happened?*

Brett raised his head and turned to me, his face contorted with pain and anger. "He killed her just as sure as if he'd put a gun to her head. When I told him she was going off with me, he said 'I'd rather see her dead!' Well, he *did* see her dead!"

Suddenly Brett stood up, knocking the chair over backwards, and staggered over to me. He grabbed my wrist. I tried to twist away from him, but his fingers tightened cruelly.

"You're living with a murderer!" he hissed.

"No!" I gasped, struggling to pry his fingers off my wrist with my other hand.

"Yes! I've got no witness, but I've lived with this all these years and now you can live with it, too!"

I tried to reach for the riding crop I'd laid on the table, but before I could reach it, a paroxysm of coughing overtook him and he dropped my hand as he hunched forward.

I took the chance to make my escape. Picking up my crop, I ran for the door and down the steps, my boots clattering on the wooden boards. Panting, I untied Missy's reins, somehow got myself up and into the saddle, whirled her around and raced down the road.

The light rain had turned to icy drizzle. It pelted my head and back as I huddled over Missy's neck. I had left my riding gloves on Brett's table when I ran out, and the wet leather reins cut into my bare palms. Daylight was fading fast. I still had a long way to go before reaching the safe haven of the barn at Bon Chance.

My hair slipped out of my snood, my hat

fell back and soon my hair was soaked. It was hard to see through the driving rain, but Missy knew her way once we reached the ridge and started for home.

Back on Montrose property now and heading for the barn, I saw the figures of two men holding lanterns, while a horse was being led out. As we approached I recognized the man standing ready to mount was Randall.

He spun around as I pulled to a stop in front of him. He was at Missy's side in an instant, one hand on her bridle, the other grabbing for the reins. In the wavering lantern light, I could see the combined fury and fear in his face.

"Where have you been? I was just starting out to look for you!"

Holding back the half-sob of relief I felt at being safely home, I didn't answer. I was drenched and shivering with cold. He put up his hands and lifted me out of the saddle.

"You little fool, you should have known better than to ride so far and stay out this long," he said grimly.

My legs were shaking and I leaned against him for a moment. I felt his arms go around me, holding me hard. Then I pulled away and pushed the strands of wet hair out of my eyes. We stared at each other for a long second, then I brushed past him and started in a half-run to the house. Behind me, I heard Randall issuing brisk orders to rub Missy down, see that she was fed.

Once in the house I went upstairs, so drained and weary I had to cling to the banister. At the top Vinny stood waiting, her eyes wide with fright.

"Oh, Miss, Mr. Bondurant was in a fierce temper about you! I ain't never seed him lak that . . . not since the night Miss Alair —"

Vinny's arm went around my waist and she guided me along the hall to my bedroom. Of course, that's why Randall seemed so angry. He was thinking of Alair.

Vinny stripped the soaking wet jacket and heavy riding skirt from my shivering body while the frightened housemaid poured kettles of boiling water into the large copper tub Vinny had pulled in front of the roaring fire in the fireplace. I got out of my underclothes and stepped into the soothing warmth of the hot water, leaned my head back against the rim, closed my eyes. Every bone in my body ached, every muscle knotted. But soon I began to relax, gradually felt revived.

After awhile, Vinny held out a blanket she had heated for me. "Best you git out now, Miss Dru, 'fore the water turns cool."

She wrapped me in the blanket, then seated herself on the stool in front of the fire and gently dried my feet, slipped on warm stockings, and helped me into my flannel nightie and quilted robe.

"I'm goin' go get some hot coals to put in the warmin' pan and get your bed nice and cozy," she told me as she hurried out of the room.

I moved over to the dressing table, picked up the brush to brush my damp hair. It seemed almost too heavy.

My meeting with Brett had been a harrowing experience, and I was still feeling its effects. If what he had told me was true, no wonder Randall was upset! Tonight's circumstances must have reminded him sharply of the night Alair died. Yet, if Brett were telling the truth, Randall had followed her out to the woods to prevent her running away. I shuddered, imagining the scene he had described.

On the other hand, the story I had heard was that Alair's horse had returned to the barn, riderless. *Then* Randall had found her. If Brett's story were true, Randall would have had to leave Alair lying mortally injured, return to the house, pretend anxiety for her, then go looking for her.

I couldn't believe that! That was too awful!

Brett's story was so tainted with ugliness, so sordid, so unlike anything I had really suspected. I hated to think my cousin, as irresponsible and flighty as she may have been, would have broken her marriage vows, abandoned her children, and run away with Brett Tolliver. I shrank from this version of the story, as well.

I put my head in my hands, wishing I had never pursued the rumors or tried to unravel the mystery.

I felt a strange emptiness and wondered when the numbness would wear off and the pain would begin. If Brett were telling the truth, there was no hope of a life or love with Randall Bondurant.

A knock at my bedroom door interrupted my depressing thoughts.

Thinking it was Vinny, I called out, "Come in."

In the mirror, I could see that it was Randall, carrying a steaming mug on a small tray.

"I brought you a hot toddy. Drink all of it. It will ward off a chill," he said, setting it down on the dressing table beside me. He stood back and, by lifting my eyes, I could see him without turning around.

"I'm sorry if I sounded angry. It's just that I was worried . . . afraid something had happened to you."

I saw him lift his hand as if to stroke my hair, then he took a few steps away from me.

I picked up the mug with both hands, inhaled the rich lemony scent rising with the steam.

"If I weren't sure of my feelings before, Dru, this afternoon convinced me," Randall said stiffly. "Don't ever scare me like that again . . . I care too much . . . I — I love you."

How ironic, I thought. I had been secretly in love with Randall Bondurant for months. Now I had to ask myself if I could really love the man who had caused my cousin's death.

I could ignore it all. Forget what Brett Tolliver had told me this afternoon. Pretend there had been no letters. Close my eyes to evidence, shut my mind to doubts. Listen only to my heart's secret yearning.

But my need for truth was compelling.

I got out of bed, pulled open the dressing table drawer, gathered up the pile of anonymous notes I'd hidden there and, clutching them in my hand, spun around and held them out to Randall.

"Here!" I said. "This is why I rode out to the Tollivers' place. To ask Brett Tolliver the truth about Alair's death!"

I watched the color drain from Randall's face. "Brett Tolliver!" he exclaimed bitterly. "He doesn't know the meaning of truth. Why would you go to him? Why not ask me?"

I was silent in the face of his rage. "He said you were responsible for Alair's death. That you left her for dead when she fell from her horse." I spoke in a monotone, giving him room to react honestly.

"He told you *that?"*

"Yes."

"And you believed him?"

My voice broke a little. "I — don't know what to believe. That's why I went."

Randall grabbed the notes from my hand. His eyes raced over them, dropping them one by one on the floor.

"Lies! All lies." He strode to the door, crumpling the bits of paper underfoot, then whirled around and came toward me, standing over me. Frightened I shrank back.

"You had only to ask me, Dru. I would have told you. I have nothing to hide. What else did Brett tell you? Did he tell you he never let Alair alone from the day we were married? As long as we were in Virginia, he was slinking around. That's why we traveled so much.

"He couldn't bear for anyone else to be happy when he was so miserable, and she *was* happy with me — for a short time anyhow. But Brett pursued her relentlessly, sent her letters, stalked her when she went riding in the woods."

His voice hushed, he paused, white-knuckled fists revealing his emotional pain. "Alair and I . . . had talked of going to Europe. She loved the south of France. We were making plans to rent a house there when Brett wrote a note, insisting that he see her. I didn't want her to go that afternoon . . . begged her not to, in fact. Our marriage was not perfect . . . I'm not pretending it was . . . and Alair was headstrong. But we both wanted to make our marriage work . . . because of the children. We thought . . . in France . . . we could put our differences aside, start over —"

Randall shrugged. "A foolish idea, I suppose, but there it was. Anyway, she told me she would tell Brett once and for all to stop trying to see her, to get on with his life, find someone and make his own happiness. She said they were childhood friends, he would listen to her. Of course, he didn't. I think he tried to force her to come with him, and she tried to escape. He was frightened and left when he saw she was dead. I think that's what really happened . . . though, unfortunately, I can't prove it." Randall's shoulders slumped.

The room was suddenly still. I hardly dared breathe.

"Since then, I think Brett has deluded himself that it happened the way he told you. That relieves him of any guilt. The man lives in an alcoholic fog most of the time. I think it's his escape from the hell he's created for himself."

Randall turned and looked at me steadily. "And *that is* the truth, Dru. I became alarmed when Alair did not return within a reasonable time, so I saddled up and was starting out to look for her when her horse came back alone." He threw out his hands in a helpless gesture. "You know the rest. It's up to you whom you believe."

The silence stretched between us. Then Randall said, "Either you trust me or you don't. But without trust . . . there is no hope for love."

I saw the muscle tightening along his jawline. He waited for me to speak, but I was too overcome with emotion. The long day's events had depleted my strength.

Slowly Randall turned and walked out of the room.

I leaned weakly back against the dressing table, then turned, put my elbows on the top, and covered my face with my hands. As I did so, I knocked over the Dresden figurine Randall had given me for Christmas. It shattered into a million pieces.

With a gasp of dismay, I picked up one of the pieces of porcelain and burst into tears. Could it ever be mended, restored? Or was it damaged as irrevocably as my relationship with Randall seemed to be?

chapter
25

When I finally went to sleep, I slept the sleep of the exhausted. I awoke to find Vinny standing at the foot of my bed.

"Oh, Miss Dru, I'm so glad to see you 'wake. I been in here two or three times and you never stirred. The children most anxious to see you. They wuz dat worried 'bout you last night."

Vinny went over to the windows and drew back the curtains, admitting a stream of sunlight.

"It's a real pretty day, Miss Dru. But Mr. Bondurant, he think you better stay in bed and rest today after yo' bad 'sperience yestiddy."

I raised myself on my elbows. "There's no need for me to do that, Vinny. I'm perfectly fine," I said, but when I tried to get up I felt the stiffness of sore muscles and eased myself back on my pillows.

"Now I'll go see 'bout your breakfast tray, Miss Dru. You jes' stay put." Vinny came over and plumped up the pillows behind my back, helping me into a more comfortable position.

The unusual hard riding, the stress of my encounter with Brett, getting chilled in the rain — all must be having an effect. It did feel good to lie quietly in the soft warm bed and be waited on for a change.

In addition, I was not ready to face Randall. Keeping to my room today would give me a chance to sort out the tangled threads of our lives.

At the door Vinny asked, "Can the children come in? Dey out here sittin' on de top of de steps."

"Oh, yes, Vinny! Tell them I want to see them!"

In a minute both little girls came running in. Lally threw herself on the bed into my arms, and Nora came next, more gently.

"Are you all right, Drucie?" she asked anxiously.

"Yes, darling, I'm fine," I reassured her.

Lally cuddled close to me. "We missed you, Drucie. We thought you were lost in the forest . . . like Hansel and Gretel!" Her dark eyes were wide but sparkled with mischief.

I gave her a squeeze, then reached for

Nora's hand. "I did a silly thing. I rode too far and got caught in the rain. Something you two better never try!" I shook my finger at them playfully.

"Papa was very upset, Drucie," Nora said solemnly.

"I know, and I'm sorry I worried everyone."

"We love you, Drucie, that's why," Lally said, nodding her head. "When you love someone, you cry if anything bad happens to them."

I pulled her closer. "Well, nothing bad happened and I learned a good lesson. Now, tell me about what you've been learning with Jed," I changed the subject.

When Vinny brought my tray, I shared my toast and jam with them as we chatted happily. Looking at their bright little faces, listening to their childish talk, a fierce, protective love sprang up within me that was as natural as if they had been born to me. I knew I would never let any harm come to them, whatever it took.

After they ran off to get ready for their riding lesson, the warmth of my feeling for them lingered. With it came the conviction that above all else *that* was the bond that held Randall and me together.

Angry as he had seemed last night, he

must know that what I had done was out of my desire to protect him and his children from the malicious slander Brett was spreading. Now I was sure of the truth. In my heart, I knew Randall to be incapable of doing what Brett had said — leaving Alair for dead.

The story Brett had told me was false. I was sure now. Over the years, his bitterness had become an obsession fueled by disappointment, rejection, and alcohol.

Suddenly, it seemed imperative that I assure Randall that I believed him. The look of outrage on his face when I had confronted him still disturbed me. I would have to apologize, try to explain why I needed to end my doubts, once and for all.

Dear Lord, I hope it isn't too late! I whispered as I got out of bed, dressed. Something told me to hurry.

As I came down the stairs I saw the confirmation of that inner prompting. Lined up at the front door as if for departure stood Randall's leather traveling bags.

I suppose my shock showed on my face when Randall, coming from his wing of the house, saw me standing at the foot of the steps.

"I thought it best if I went away for a few days," he said briskly, turning his handsome, elegant profile from me, slapping his gloves several times into the palm of his other hand. I realized he had not anticipated seeing me before he left.

Instead of grief at the thought of his leaving, I felt indignation. There was unfinished business between us. It ought to be settled now before the rift my doubts had caused between us became a chasm, an impassable bridge.

"Best for whom?" I asked.

He seemed surprised by my question. "For — for all of us."

"You think running away will help?" I demanded.

Randall's face flushed, his dark eyes snapped. He was not used to being challenged.

"Running away? I'm not running away."

"Aren't you?" I countered. "I believe you are afraid to find out the truth. I could have run from it, too. I was afraid of what I might find, but I didn't try to escape."

"And now that you've found — the truth — or at least what you think is the truth — what now?" Randall was looking at me steadily.

"That's what I came to tell you," I said. "But it seems you don't want to hear." I started past him, but he reached out, caught my arm, and swung me back to face him.

"Whatever you've got to say, I want to hear it."

I looked into that face I'd come to love, the intensity of the dark eyes that held both fear and hope and my heart responded.

"Say it. I'm not afraid," Randall said fiercely.

"I believe you. I love you." I heard my own voice speak the words I had never dared say before.

In another moment I was in his arms. He was holding me so close I could smell the starch of his ruffled shirt, the expensive cologne he used, feel his heart pounding against mine.

"Oh, my dearest," Randall murmured. "Dearest Dru."

I felt joyous tears rush into my eyes as I clung to him, but laughter, too, bubbled up inside. I was filled with a kind of giddy happiness.

Gently Randall released me, held me a little way from him and gazed at me intently. "You're sure?"

"Very sure," I replied, smiling.

His hands framed my face, held it for a fraction of a second, then leaning forward, he kissed me gently. I closed my eyes, feeling as if the world were spinning, yet strangely secure in those strong, firm hands. When I opened my eyes, it was all still there — Randall, looking at me with infinite love and tenderness, the hallway shimmering with golden light.

Suddenly we heard giggles and we both turned to see two little faces pressed between the stair railings from the balcony above.

We looked at each other, then hand-in-hand went to the bottom of the stairway and stretched out our arms. Nora and Lally came tumbling down to be enclosed in our embrace.

That evening, after the children were in bed, Randall and I sat together in the firelight of the library and talked for hours. We spoke of the pattern of events that had brought about our present happiness.

"God works in mysterious ways," Randall said seriously. "You came into my life — our lives — when I needed you most. You brought light and love where there had been so much darkness. Most of all, you brought hope. Hope that life could again have meaning. I'll always be grateful. Every day of my life, I'll get down on my knees and thank God for bringing this 'wonder' to me."

I had never heard Randall speak like this and I was very touched.

"For a time, it seemed as if I lost my childhood faith. I was embittered by my father's unremitting anger at what was a youthful misstep at worst. Then I grew rebellious. Filled with anger. I wanted to prove I didn't need him or inherited money to succeed. And I went about it in ways I'm not very proud of now."

"All that's in the past now, Randall, we have the future to think of, to plan for, and it will be wonderful," I promised. "A whole new life."

He reached over and stroked my cheek. "With you, Druscilla, everything will be new."

But we were not quite yet free of the past.

A few days later on my way to the corral to watch Nora and Lally practice their jumps, I saw a rickety wagon with an old black driver come slowly up the road. I stopped and waited until he reined. He tipped his hat and brought out an envelope from his shabby jacket pocket.

" 'Noon, Missus Bondurant," he said. "This here letter is from Mr. Tolliver. He done tole me to bring it ober sooner, but my wagon wheel was broke and warn't fixed 'til today." He held out the letter to me.

Were we never to be free? Was there no end to Brett Tolliver's persecution?

"Too bad 'bout Mr. Tolliver, Missus. He were a fine gemmelmen 'till he took to drinkin'," the man said as he turned the wagon around.

His words did not register at once. When they did, I ran after the wagon, calling, "Stop! Please stop! What do you mean? What's wrong with Mr. Tolliver?"

"He done died in his sleep last week, ma'am. Docta say he doan' know whether 'twas whiskey or pneumonia that done it."

Brett Tolliver dead!

I felt both enormous relief and extreme compassion. Relief that the menace threatening our happiness was removed, compassion for a life that had been both anguished and wasted.

I opened the envelope then and saw what was scribbled there.

LIES ALL LIES. R.B. NOT GUILTY. MAY GOD HAVE MERCY ON MY SOUL. FORGIVE ME WHAT I DID.

Brett's signature was scrawled in shaky letters.

I clasped my hands over the paper and bowed my head and prayed for that poor man that he might at last find peace.

Then I started walking toward the corral again. I could see the girls on their ponies and Randall, leaning over the fence, watching them. As I drew near, he saw me and waved.

Then he held out his arms, and I ran to embrace my destiny!

Epilogue

September 1885

Dear Jonathan,

By the time you receive this letter, you and Davida will have just returned from your honeymoon. Aunt Garnet told us she was the most beautiful bride and you the handsomest groom she had ever seen. I wish I could have been there to see for myself and to wish you both as great happiness in your marriage as I have found in mine.

Did you know Randall and I repeated our wedding vows in a second ceremony? It was very private, with only Mama, Auntie Kate Cameron, and the two little girls in attendance. Uncle Rod did the honors of "giving me away" to Randall!

Why a second ceremony?

You see, in Rome, we were only able to arrange a civil ceremony, which seemed the farthest thing from a real wedding to me. When I explained this to Randall, he was only too willing to have another, one more to my liking.

Can you guess where it was? Do you remember the little chapel on the grounds at Montclair — the one our ancestress Avril had built to accommodate the many traveling preachers she entertained through the years? It is the sweetest place inside, with an arched roof, latticed windows, a tiny altar and pulpit, and a half dozen pews on either side of the short aisle.

For Davida's information (and I suspect by now you are learning how dearly women crave to know what was worn on such occasions!), I wore a hyacinth-blue ensemble — Randall's favorite color — and one of my precious Paris bonnets of scalloped straw, trimmed with blue ribbons and satin roses.

The little girls were my bridesmaids and wore batiste dresses with hyacinth-blue sashes and straw hats, wreathed with cornflowers.

Enough of this high fashion and on to the more important purpose of this letter.

There is much to tell you of the events that have taken place since I last wrote. You will note the postmark on the envelope is Charleston, South Carolina.

As you know, Randall had been estranged from his family for many years. His father disowned him and Randall had had no contact with either his mother or sister since.

Recently, he received word of his father's death and a letter from his mother in which she expressed her longing to be re-united. She also stated she felt Mr. Bondurant had regretted his hasty action against his only son, but was too proud to rescind it.

As a result, we immediately made plans to visit Randall's mother at the family home near Charleston. There, Nora and Lally found themselves welcomed by a loving grandmother, an aunt, and some cousins. We spent a most happy two weeks there.

The main reason for this letter is that Randall and I, after long discussions, have made some decisions that will affect you and your future.

Since Mrs. Bondurant is elderly and not knowledgeable of the business affairs of her late husband, a cotton broker, Randall has agreed to take over the management of his firm, until such time as it can be profit-ably sold.

We are moving to Pokeberry Plantation on Sullivan's Island, the Bondurant summer place, to be near his mother while Randall settles the estate.

We both agree that it is unlikely that we will ever live in Virginia again. In Charleston, the Bondurants are an old, established family and here the girls will have an assured entré into society. In fact, Mrs. Bondurant and her daughter, Amelia, are already talking about their making their debut at the St. Cecilia Ball when they are eighteen!

Therefore, we have deeded Bon Chance to you. As Uncle Malcolm's son, you are the rightful heir, and since it has been completely restored to its former splendid condition, you and Davida can come here to find it as it was when your dear mother arrived as a bride.

I hope this makes you as happy as it made us to arrange it. You will soon receive all the legal papers, clearly outlining all the provisions. When you sign them, Montclair will be yours!

In conclusion, my dearest cousin, I want to tell you the real reason I could not travel so far North to be with you on the most joyous day of your life. It is for "happy conditions of health." Yes, Randall and I are expecting an addition to our little family. I am praying it will be a son to carry on the Bondurant heritage.

I cannot wish a more sincere or happier hope that you and Davida, in time, will know a similar expectation and that Montclair will again have its own Montrose heir. God bless and keep you both.

> With devoted love, always,
> Your affectionate cousin,
> Dru